*Seven Against Georgia*

# EDUARDO MENDICUTTI

# Seven
# Against
# Georgia

## Erotic Fiction

*Translated from the Spanish by Kristina Cordero*

Grove Press
New York

*Published simultaneously in Canada*
*Printed in the United States of America*

FIRST EDITION

Library of Congress Cataloging-in-Publication Data
Mendicutti, Eduardo, 1948–
[Siete contra Georgia. English]
Seven against Georgia : erotic fiction / by Eduardo Mendicutti ;
translated from the Spanish by Kristina Cordero.
p. cm.
ISBN 0-8021-4037-8
I. Cordero, Kristina.   II. Title.
PQ6663.E49S5413 2003
863'.64—dc21      2003049078

Grove Press
841 Broadway
New York, NY 10003

03 04 05 06 07   10 9 8 7 6 5 4 3 2 1

To the policemen of the State of Georgia

To my friends, in the hope that they take
this with a sense of humor

# Contents

## *II*

## *III*

## *IV*

## *V*

*Seven Against Georgia*

# Prologue

*Where Miss Boccaccio introduces
a group of wayward women and
defends their individual rights to seek
pleasure any which way they can*

That horny tramp Mercurio came to me one day, completely out of control, and said,

"Sweetheart, you better sit down, I've got news." And I said,

"Baby, the only sweetheart you've got is your daddy, you sonofabitch."

And he said,

"Go to hell, you little queer."

As you can see, quite the intellectual conversation.

Of course, that was only the introduction to the story, to be followed by body, climax, and conclusion.

"Miss Balcony has called me," said Mercurio. "In that god-awful screeching voice of hers. What a mouth she's got on her—I'm still shaking from the shivers it gives me. Anyway, that little degenerate left me the most unbelievable mes-

sage. Get this: she's in her house, completely immobilized
in a plaster cast, completely hysterical, with her left tibia
completely out of commission, plaster down to her toes,
down to the very tips of her toenails, and she says that if
her friends don't come and see her on the double she's going
to have a conniption."

That was all, if you can picture it. Of course, I recognize that Mercurio is quite accustomed to deciphering the
deluge of semitelegraphic messages she receives. That, after
all, is her business and, one would assume, her specialty. And
precisely for this reason—the tone of Miss Balcony's voice,
her obvious anxiety, the babbling manner in which she told
the tale—Mercurio assured me that this one was going to
be worth it:

"Listen, pussycat, this is Mercurio talking. This is going
to be good."

Mercurio, just so you know, is the answering machine
for the telephone number 272-3447. I suppose you've gath-
ered by now what an outrageous queer she is. And deviant,
too. She claims that all those messages infected her, as if
deviance were scarlet fever or something. Now listen, I'm
going to tell you something, and this is in the strictest confidence: the truth is, her real problem is that her cunt has
been ripped to shreds because she knows she's old and
rudimentary, an obsolete, primitive machine. That's the way
she came into this world, so don't blame it on me, it's not
my fault.

And me? Why, I'm innocence personified. Truly. Well,
in reality I'm a tape recorder, but as far as I'm concerned,

that has nothing to do with anything. Those are the facts. I'm the innocent one in all this. For the record, I am a serious, solid, well-balanced tape recorder, with one little manufacturing error: I take my batteries from behind. That, my friends, is why that batty bitch Mercurio calls me Boccaccio.

Total hearsay, I swear. What I mean is that the little viper has no proof that I like it up the ass. Yes, fine, every so often I let myself go and talk like a bitch, but that's a question of environment. I have never given Mercurio any reason at all to assume all the things she chooses to assume about me; anyway, I always shut her up. Supposedly, according to her, she can tell that I get this sick little thrill when they put the batteries in. Now, I will neither confirm nor deny that, but I will point out that it would be logical and natural, a perfectly understandable reaction of the organism, a strategically located nervous reflex, and a very normal, natural response. And if you insist, I would even say it's physiological. But my psychological makeup is completely masculine, and Mercurio has no right at all to treat me the way she does. Again, for the record, I am a portable tape recorder, battery-powered, made by a Japanese manufacturer of somewhat questionable quality, brought in through Tenerife, in the Canary Islands, and sold on the black market during the Mae West days. But I turned out fabulous. I've never given my owner—who is also Mercurio's owner, as you may have guessed by now—the least bit of trouble. My owner's nom de guerre, so to speak, is Madelon, and her telephone is cited above, just in case anyone is inspired by her fetching, tempting name. As you might also imagine . . . well, don't even bother imagining, I'll tell you right now—I am an essential element in my owner's professional life, for she is quite an artist in her field. I am the mirror image of her voice, the reflection of her soul, the weaver of her artistry. Without me, my owner would be just another drag queen hanging out on some Madrid street corner.

Anyway, Mercurio's real problem is that she's jealous. Jealous as a bitch in heat. Mercurio is just an answering machine—the old kind, and I know my answering machines. I've seen some splendid models in my time—ones with rewind, remote control, and off-site access capabilities. Mercurio, poor fool that she is, is simply prehistoric, even though she fancies herself a modern-day Dorothy Parker. A second-rate message recorder is what she is, abominable play-back quality and an altogether typical, passive machine, even though she thinks she is *sooo* macho. Who does she think she's kidding? Mercurio likes to receive, she might as well stop fooling herself. And then she prolongs the messages something awful—you can tell that she doesn't feel a thing when she gives it; that old hack is completely frigid from the front. But when she gets it from behind, the bitch spills it like a tidal wave hitting the Costa del Sol. Take it from me, you can't even imagine how her little prick gives out when someone else sticks it to her, the little sicko.

She doesn't deserve that kind of luck, I'm telling you. And what I don't understand is why she insists on denying it. Maybe she thinks—oh, she is so misguided—that back-door delights are second-class pleasures. The poor thing is so provincial, I'm telling you.

And me? When they shove those batteries inside of me, I feel like I'm being serenaded by the entire *Lucia ∂i Lammermoor* opera.

So you get the idea, more or less, right? Mercurio creams her panties when she gets it from behind but she lacks refinement. And sadly, there is no changing her now. To add insult to injury, that pretentious bitch is constantly insinuating that she is far more important to our owner than me. Stark, raving mad, I tell you.

And then she has the nerve to tell me, "Modern life is so fast-paced, so insane, that an answering machine means more to an artist nowadays than her own mother. Than her own mother and her manager put together."

And that's not all: "The automatic answering machine, baby, belongs to the video generation; the tape recorder, to the TV movie era."

The poor thing is *so* ignorant.

A servant whose job is to take messages, that's what she is. No initiative. No feeling. Hopelessly passive, anyone can see that. I, on the other hand, always tell my owner the truth. I reproduce her artistry exactly as it is, not how she imagines it to be, and when one of her numbers is still a bit green, and I tell it to her in good faith in her own voice, every time she rehearses, when she emotes, practices her jokes, or tries out some song without relying on the help of lip-synching. Darlings, my owner only *listens* to Mercurio. She *trusts* me.

Excuse me. I just called you "darlings." A slip of the tongue. Well, I suppose that's a sign of the bond I feel between us. Now listen, I'm going to tell you something, if I might be so bold: don't kid yourselves, we're all the same. If you were a tape recorder and people stuck batteries up your ass, you'd love it too.

    More than once, in our better days, Mercurio and I discussed it. And we concluded that in this field, you simply have to try everything, and let heaven and Lana Turner be the judge of right and wrong. But Mercurio, of course, always thinks that the dominant queer is the more important actor in this little play, and that's why she's always running around mouthing off about what a macho bitch she is. It's pure nonsense, of course, and I've told her so a thousand times, though I'm not always so obnoxious about it. Because, obviously, I don't want you to think that Mercurio and I spend all day at each other's throats. Of course we don't—exactly the opposite, in fact. You might say that we're condemned to understand each other. What other choice do we have? We spend all our waking hours side by side—and maybe, just maybe, our problem is that we never got it on, as we probably should have by now. There we sit, just the two of us, on the night table, all alone, all day long. For God's sake, you'd get friendly with a hyena under these conditions. And I can tell she's got her eye on me, not just because of all the things I've told you about, but also because I get to travel a little, and she never goes anywhere. Sometimes Madelon takes me out of the house, to go on tour, or to visit talent agencies with a few elegant, discreet cassettes featuring selected recordings of some of her numbers, some of them taped live with the roar of the crowd in the background, you know, for effect. Really, if the situation were reversed, I would resent Mercurio a little, so I understand where she's coming from.

As such, I fully understand why she sits in Miss Balcony's house fuming over all the divine work I got to do over at Miss Balcony's house. And it was divine, I admit it, but they did work me like a dog.

You see, they had to keep Miss Balcony entertained. My owner took care of that one immediately. Miss Balcony left five messages with Mercurio before Madelon could return the call. Mercurio was fit to be tied—all she kept saying, all afternoon, was that this crazy faggot has got some story to tell. "And you heard it from Mercurio first," she said. Judging by the five messages, Miss Balcony was a regular basket case. At wits' end. She kept saying that her cherry was sore from so much use. That her tongue was wagging down like a dog's, desperate to refresh her cunt with a little fresh saliva. That her nerves were wound up as tight as the Jockey shorts of a sailor on shore leave.

When Madelon finally arrived home and called her, the only thing Miss Balcony would say was this:

"Come over. Right now. I can't take it a minute longer. I have to tell you everything."

So you can see the state of affairs: if it hadn't been for me, Mercurio would have gotten only half the story. And to think she has the nerve to compare herself to Boccaccio. Such a lack of humility, my God. You'd think she'd know her place by now.

To be honest, the whole story was rather confusing at first, for both of us. Madelon, my owner, didn't come home

until the wee hours of the morning—it was her night off at
the Contramano—but by nine in the morning she was up
again, talking on the telephone like a woman possessed. Of
course, at that hour, the nocturnal escapades of Madrid
hadn't yet made it to the goddamn answering machines.
Their conversations were brief and cryptic; obviously they
had spoken the day before, when my owner was at Miss
Balcony's house. Of those early-morning conversations, the
final comment was always the same:

"Don't fail us now, baby. Those gringos had better hear
us out. They're going to hear us. In Spanish, baby, in Spanish. They're rich—they can afford translators. And they're
old, some of them as old as the hills. You just watch what's
going to go down. Poor Miss Balcony—the Virgin Mary
didn't suffer half as much. You'll see. A great big faggoty
mess; what a disaster. All because of four stupid little boys
who are actually serious about that sermon handed down
by Reagan's old hag or whatever the hell her name is, that
frigid bitch in the Supreme Court. But they're going to hear
us out, because they have no other choice, baby. So don't
fail us now, or I'll sew you up for good, you little queer.
Afternoon tea is on me today, baby. After that, we can all
take turns. And the tape recorder is on me too."

That's what she said, almost word for word, one call
after the other, to the group of wayward ladies whose names
I present to you below.

Herr Betty Honey.

Colette la Coco, also known as Miss Polaroid.

Finita Languedoc, occasionally known as Miss Luxe.

Pamela Poodle, also known, in intimate circles, as Miss Walking Disaster. And finally,

Veronica Switchblade.

With Miss Balcony and Madelon, that makes seven.

And that was how I spent seven days in Miss Balcony's house. Listening to each and every one of them. Once Miss Madelon finished giving her instructions, she tidied up the house a bit, and took me aside.

"All right," she said. "Let's see how you work this one, faggot, because you're going to have to perform a little terrorism—*sexual* terrorism, don't have a cow. Let's see how many retrograde gringos we can send into cardiac arrest."

Mercurio, as you might imagine, didn't get it. Not at all. I barely had time to explain it to her:

"Listen, baby, the gringo powers-that-be have decided that sucking off and taking it up the ass is against the law, and has to be punished. Because of this, apparently, Miss Balcony is going to be sent up the river. And these crazy bitches want to take justice into their own hands."

Will it work? That, my friends, remains to be seen. For the moment, the results are in your hands: seven stories, seven explosive cassettes. And to start, my owner is going to send these seven cassettes, like one giant letter bomb, sent by certified return-receipt mail, to the chief of police of the State of Georgia.

# I

*Where Miss Balcony attempts, despite her multiple bruises and multiple digressions, to convince a rather incredulous audience of the aphrodisiac properties found in a loaf of bread*

Dear Mr. Police Chief of the State of Georgia: get comfortable now, press down on your sphincter, arrange your jewels so they don't bother you, and fasten your seat belt, just like Bette Davis said. Miss Balcony is my name, and consider yourself lucky that the rules of this game prohibit me from insulting you, because otherwise you'd find out just what Miss Balcony's little golden spout is capable of spewing forth. But that, sir, is prohibited. I must obey the rules, and my fabulous queer sisters are already telling me enough with the introductions, the tape is rolling.

Baby, even the tape recorder is a member of this union: they call her Boccaccio. Well, all right, forget the "baby" bit, these bitches are telling me to move on and just hit you with my best shot.

Here goes. Now, before getting into specifics I should
explain the story behind my name, Miss Balcony. You probably won't believe it, but anyway. This humble servant is
an architect—okay, so it took me nine years to get the de-
gree, but believe me, I've got plenty of imagination and good
taste to boot. Wait, wait, these bitches are getting on my case
again. Go for the jugular already, they're telling me. Now,
as you might have guessed, I owe my nom de guerre to them:
I live right smack in the Plaza de España—note the choice
address, I wouldn't want you to think that all us fabulous
queers are dying of hunger. Fuck it, let me embellish a
little—because the Plaza de España is the caviar of Madrid,
and when it comes to European cities we all know that
Madrid is bad, so very bad. In this town you boys would
put on your boots and fill up your jail in ten seconds with
all the ladies we've got here, some of them quite elegant, take
my word for it—like me, for example. Now, Miss Balcony
has an apartment you would die for in the Plaza de España—
relax, relax, I want to give the boy an idea of the design
scheme—completely renovated, like new. The apartment,
I mean—my cunt is a total disaster, everyone in Madrid
knows that, who am I kidding? With all the characters that
have crossed my threshold by now, it's a well-known fact
that my cunt is located out back. But that, shall we say, is a
geographic accident, as much as you and your boys may
refuse to believe.

All right, girls, I get the picture. They're nagging me
to get to the point. Very well, I will try to tell you my story
as briefly as I know how. There I was, walking home from

the Plaza de Callao, on foot, like a bitch in heat. And just as
I stroll past a movie theater showing a soft-core porn flick,
an adorable boy walks out, the kind you just don't see much
of anymore: a gorgeous construction-worker type, blond but
with dark skin, taller than me, tight pecs, hard little nipples,
arms like tree trunks, hands like a lumberjack and just in
case you don't catch the drift, honey, the package on this
guy only barely made it into his jeans. And the way he was
walking, pumped up and hard as a rock, struggling in vain
against a bulge that was as swollen as the Sunday paper, it
made you feel sorry for the poor thing—he was about to
explode. Oh, what pain, what anguish—mine, that is. Just
looking at him made me want to cry, and immediately I
began to pray like crazy that I wouldn't faint and fall into a
coma right there on the street. No way could I let this one
get away, I would never forgive myself. He looked ready to
come; he could barely walk, with the hard-on he had. His
body seemed almost numb, frantic, and from the creases in
his pants you could just picture the cock he had on him, it
was enough to make you scream. I went wild just looking
at him, and then my eyes started stinging and my asshole
started to quiver. What a scandalously fabulous package he
had, for God's sake, so perfectly silhouetted against his
thigh. . . . Oh, the palpitations, oh, the tremors it gave me.
That man was dangerous; he was on the verge of a heart
attack, he was so desperate to spill his load. He needed help,
he needed release, full release, and he had to have noticed
how I was staring at him. And when I stare, it's for real. My
stares are delectable enough to eat, so how could he not

notice? Well, of course he noticed—I mean, the look on my face must have been bad, out of control. I could barely swallow, my God, I couldn't take my eyes off him, so how could we help but cause a major scandal right there on the Gran Vía, with me facing him and him facing me, both of us frantic, him with his hand in his pocket, desperately trying to control his prick, and me with my panties all creamed and my throat as wide open as the arms of Mother Teresa of Calcutta. My God, at that moment my throat was open so wide it could have swallowed the entire population of India, the pyramids of Giza, the Hanging Gardens of Babylon, the Alhambra of Granada, the complete works of Pío Baroja, but most of all, the abundant offerings of that adorable creature, that masterpiece of masculinity, that stud whose tiny hole was ready to burst, he could barely stand it anymore, he wasn't going to hold out. And that's the way the poor thing looked at me, as if he was drowning, beseeching me to rescue him; I felt genuine pity for him—pity, I tell you. What a beautiful way to smile at someone; it was as if he was saying, "Do what you want with me, sonofabitch, this is a once-in-a-lifetime chance, take advantage of me now, I can barely move with the hard-on I've got." That's what the little angel was telling me with his smile and his eyes, even though he couldn't utter a single word; it was as though he feared total blowout if he dared to say or do anything. So yours truly had to take the initiative, and take it from me, yoga is worth its weight in gold, girls: I exercised restraint, total control of muscles, glands, and cartilage, maintained superior flexibility, employed my deep-breathing techniques, kept my mind in blank, slowed down the heartbeat, relaxed the internal organs — a regular Hollywood performance. But I had to watch it, I couldn't let the arousal grow soft, either, I couldn't let *anything* grow soft. Now, I am an actress, and you better believe I had to employ every last trick in the book, just so that he wouldn't see the kind of restraint I was exerting. I had to keep the sparks flying, I had to suffuse my voice with enough suggestive innuendo to give him shivers as he heard me say, so brilliantly, so intensely,

"That movie got you hard as a rock, baby." Finally, at that, he managed to nod his head yes. And then I replied,

"Easy, baby, relax a little, try to think of something else." A look of pure frustration came over his face, only for an instant, but it spoke volumes. That was when, very smoothly, I introduced myself. Naturally I gave him my real name, my baptismal name, my masculine name, because that day I was dressed like a man from head to toe. That day I was the architect, the responsible citizen. And right away I said to him,

"Why don't we go inside — it will distract you a little." We were right outside of a huge bar filled with slot machines, one of those places that could turn off the randiest faggot. But he shook his head no, as if to say, "Take those machines and stick them up your ass, honey." Then he breathed deeply, smiled to himself for strength, took his hand out of his pocket, and motioned with that hand as if to say, "Let's just keep our cool."

"My name is Anselmo," he then murmured. "Pleased to meet you." "The pleasure is all mine," I said, or at least that was what I was thinking—pleasure was exactly what I wanted to give him, pleasure like nobody had ever given him before. For the moment, however, I was unable to say a thing, and so I kept the thought to myself and went weak at the knees as he admitted that the movie had, in fact, gotten him as fired up as a brand-new Yamaha. To be honest, I don't remember if he said Yamaha or Honda or what—I don't know much about motorcycles, but I can assure you that Anselmo was a full-cylinder, top-of-the-line model, what with all those cubic meters the movie had piled onto his frame. The movie wasn't even that good, he said, but added,

"I've been existing on bread and water for God only knows how long, if you know what I mean. It's been ages since my last little taste treat, you know? Occupational hazard, I guess, sir." Good God, how I love it when men with rock-hard cocks call me "sir," I love it when a stud starts off like that, so full of respect, only to end up giving me a tongue-lashing like a streetwalker as he comes, as he fills me up with his sweet, sticky yogurt. And I felt myself grow woozy as I fantasized about the kind of pantry that horny ram would have stored away after so much fasting in the interest of his professional obligations. And then I asked him: "What *is* your profession, anyway?" That was when he admitted that he worked in Villaverde, at the National Guard academy for noncommissioned officers. I almost had seven orgasms, one after the other, right there. Thank God for yoga, though, especially after what happened next. He leaned toward me and with his mouth right next to my ear whispered that he was ready to pump me up right there, hot and sweet. What an experience, my God, the miracle of yoga was the one and only thing that saved me from falling flat on my face. As I started to go weak in the knees, he put his hand around my waist and my hand couldn't help but graze the tip of his inflamed bud, why, it was just like touching heaven itself with the tips of my fingers. Suddenly I got goose bumps all over and it felt as if all my juices were about to come rushing out of my pores, and that was when he jumped back a bit.

"Careful," he warned, "let's not fuck it up now," and finally he asked me if I knew of some place we could go. Suddenly I felt like a true queen again, rich and powerful, as elegant and exclusive as the Côte d'Azur, and in the most magnanimous way I knew how I told him that I had a marvelous apartment only a few blocks away, at the end of the Gran Vía right on the Plaza de España: a penthouse, fabulous skyline views from every window. Of course, he could have cared less about the view, but image sells, girls, and in the end the urban landscape did take on a certain significance in this little episode. The whole way there I was petrified that this answer to my prayers wouldn't be fulfilled in the most ideal circumstances, because it had already been quite a stroll and my archangel had to walk half bowlegged to avoid causing any unnecessary friction that would threaten to end it all on our way upstairs, and God only knows that the hum of the elevator was enough to drive me mad as I worried that it was all for naught and feared that he was going to explode on me right there. But as luck would have it, he distracted himself somehow. Suddenly, he asked me why there were so many people in the plaza looking up. I explained that a group of trapeze artists had stretched a steel cable from the plaza floor up to the top of the Edificio España building, and that a guy on a motorcycle performed a stunt of going up and down the cable. He didn't believe me and, like an idiot, I said,

"Don't worry, you'll see." And so, upon entering the house he went straight to the balcony. I placed my hand on the crack of his ass to entertain myself, my pipe on the verge of bursting, and that was when — God, what bad timing — some crazy queer announced on a loudspeaker that in a few moments some brave soul would begin the spectacle. He got all excited, because he had never seen anything like this — he was from Badajoz, and had only arrived in Madrid three months earlier. By now my floodgates were threatening to bust open, but Anselmo, damn him, was transfixed by the circus below. Then we heard the motors beginning to rev up — yes, girls, velocity and vertigo all at once. The boy from Badajoz began massaging the landmass inside his Jockey shorts, that bulbous life force beneath his jeans, the head of his prick as tense as a Republican Party meeting. . . . Ah, the quivering, the accelerated breathing, the shivers racing up and down my spine, the desperation as I bit my lips, my nose twitching, reveling in the danger of it all, Mr. Police Chief, of that man who escaped my clutches by satisfying himself on his own after such prolonged abstinence. As if I hadn't been ready and waiting for him. The man on the motorcycle solemnly rose up the cable until reaching the top of the Edificio España building, with all the windows of the nearby buildings opened wide and filled with spectators.

You have to understand, the crowd had good reason to gape, for they got a double show, two attractions for the price of one. It was like Eros and Thanatos, as the educated would say, at the same time: risk and eroticism, danger and sex, a very special performance to benefit the National Guard academy for noncommissioned officers. In midair, the man on the motorcycle was on the brink of cracking his head open, and on my balcony a humble servant was on her knees, facing that child prodigy from Badajoz on that narrow passageway. I was a bundle of nerves as I unzipped those indigo jeans that suddenly became army-green right before my eyes. I dove into the folds of a plaid shirt, scaring the flailing arms of the owner of said shirt, tearing his Jockey shorts down like a woman possessed until the light of day finally shone onto that miracle of nature, that privileged prick, that madness, that macrocock the color of corn and as thick as Fred Flintstone's forearm, straight as a rod, squeaky clean, with its smooth casing, slightly rough to the touch, with an aroma as refined and potent as the very best narcotics, an indomitable consistency, polite arrogance, as brilliant and steely as a Bergamin aphorism, as solid as a Rubén Darío poem, as tender and rebellious as a Brassens song, as sleepy as the Autumn Festival program. It was utterly irresistible and perfectly tailored to the contours of my mouth, resistant to the flow of my saliva, more than worthy of bringing my lips and tongue to the highest of altars, of catapulting my tonsils to seventh heaven. Oh, what great fortune has been bestowed upon my lips, and what a dismal fate is dealt those who will never know the joy of such a glorious Badajoz bulge sliding into the tabernacle of the throat, bathing the juices of Annunciation against a pair of gums, shining like a battalion leader's pistol against a pair of inflamed lips, flushed cheeks, and beneath the veil of a pair of eyelids, coating everything in its wake with a transparent honey that announces the great arrival, such pandemonium, such hard legs, such a tight ass, such juicy, well-proportioned balls . . . not to mention the talent of one particular lady servant, girls, and that is something I don't intend to underestimate. That man will never forget the service I rendered him, with such care, such wisdom, such momentum, such a sense of progression, such gentle games played with head and neck, even at the risk of doing harm to myself — that balcony has a stone wall that could have easily decapitated me. But risk was clearly the order of the day, for this was total indulgence. It didn't even cross my mind, or my palate, to worry about that sort of thing, for sucking away to oblivion is my personal signature — and with that glorious specimen, that flesh that tasted of victory, the nectar of the gods, *boccata di cardinale*, the pride of Badajoz. . . . Oh, how I recall that cock, how I long for its length, its thickness, its flavor, its scent, its shine. . . . Oh, how I miss it so, there is nothing I wouldn't do if he would come back to me. I would do everything in my power to lure him back, I would mobilize an army of daredevils ready to risk their lives from the top of that building on the Plaza de España, as Anselmo would rev up like a motorcycle on the balcony and I, his faithful servant, would get on my knees and risk my neck to eat his prick until my teeth fell out, until my tonsils melted away, like mountains of sugar crystals, in the richest milk I ever swallowed.

So do you understand now, Mr. Police Chief of the State of Georgia, why these degenerate queer girlfriends of mine call me Miss Balcony? Impressive, isn't it? You can have your way with me, of course. As for your cronies, they've already tried. But they can go to hell for all I care. They've left me here, in agony, with my leg in a plaster cast all the way up to my soul. And all their pricks will go soft if they don't have someone to suck them off. I'm sure you know how delectable that is. You'd have to be an idiot to declare such a delicious endeavor against the law. You may call it oral sex, if you insist on being legal about it, but around here we just call it a blow job.

Oh please, don't be so provincial — have you really never flown in a plane? Please refrain from smoking, keep your seat belts fastened until the aircraft has come to a full stop, and all that jazz? The aircraft is the airplane, just in case you didn't get that. So don't get impatient on me, we still have a long way to go. This was just a stopover, if you will, to continue with the aeronautic motif. In reality, this is a disquisition. Everything you have listened to up until now has been a kind of prelude — come on, bitches, chill out; this boy needs explanations. I recognize that I monopolized side A. But it went fast. Oh, did it go fast. My God, I barely had time to breathe. . . . What narrative flow, for goodness' sake. It's their fault, rushing me like that. The truth is that these peripatetic stories are much better when told a bit more calmly. All right, then, I will slow the pace a bit for side B.

And whoever doesn't like it can go have a cup of tea or something. Calm down. Now I am most definitely going to need my yoga for this one: yoga can work for me this time around, too, you'll see. I am going to go very, very slow; you'll see the effect is much better this way. Questions of the flesh acquire a special intensity when treated parsimoniously. And that parsimony has to be very, very good in order to tell a proper story. Let's see if I can do it. That brings me to something else: sucking off a lot gives you a strange facility for words. And if you harbor any desire to enter politics, mark my words: sucking off cultivates the oral tradition something awful. So pay attention: if your wife talks your ear off, catch a whiff of her breath. If she isn't giving it to you, she's giving it to the milkman, who's probably a young hunk with a cock to die for.

Calm down, calm down now, ladies. Me, I feel like I just took a Valium. Divine. Totally languid and glamorous. No tripping over myself like before. The story I am going to tell you now requires tranquillity and close attention to detail, so get comfortable and do some relaxation exercises.

I had a contract for a project—and anyone who says that that's some kind of miracle gets her eyes scratched out. An ideal contract—ideal, I tell you. The brother of one of my ex-lovers—oh, nobody has ever spread my cunt like that little cherub—wanted to build a house in a somewhat rundown neighborhood in an absolutely marvelous town called Sanlúcar, in the province of Cádiz; this is one place you have to make it to before you die, I swear. So he calls me and tells me that he has always felt that I have real talent as an architect—calm down, girls, don't start getting hysterical on me again; that is exactly what he said, with that same velvet voice of all the men in his family. He came to see me. Gorgeous. I only remembered him as a wee little thing, but he'd most certainly grown up to be quite big. Naturally he gave me a little demonstration before getting down to business: he asked me, with tremendous style, if I liked to be eaten out from behind, and this lady immediately lifted her ass high up. I rose to the occasion, and rested my forehead against a big pillow, so that I would be nice and comfortable for however long this one was going to take. Now, if any of you girls think you know the meaning of the words "black kiss," forget it. That man, with such manners, left me so wide open that my entire body was sore, and once he had had his way with me and got up, I said thank you, only to realize that he'd even given my vocal cords a workout. An expert, that one. It didn't even cross my mind to invite him to dinner, he had such a look of satisfaction on his face. It would have been too embarrassing to offer him a cheese omelette after that.

Then he told me, in detail, what he wanted:

"A small house, but make it original. Something that stands out. My father-in-law has given us a bit of land and I want it to look fabulous. So let your imagination run wild— I know you've got plenty of imagination—and get to work with your compass and blueprints and make me a real clever proposal. All right?"

Mr. Police Chief of the State of Georgia: can you even imagine the smooth petals my client's wife must have?

We should make a pause here, ladies, so that the boys can work up a few orgasms thinking of that little slut's tunnel, because she's a lucky one. Oh he was good, ladies. All right. I continue.

I had to move—I had no other choice. It was early spring and the air was so clean and fresh that it made you want to be a turtledove. . . . Oh, I am *so* poetic. The light was a dream. I rented a little bungalow close to the ocean, with views overlooking the Doñana nature sanctuary on the outskirts of town—it was all very ecological, mind you—and I produced a set of plans to die for. In a different league from that bland architectural garbage you see everywhere nowadays. All right, girls, all right—if there's time left over at the end I will give Mr. Policeman a concise, exact description of this masterful creation. A most delightful little house.

The contractor his father-in-law hired was, to be frank, rather vulgar—one of those men who understands nothing, for whom everything I proposed was faggy and ridiculous. So I quickly put the Neanderthal in his place and laid down my ground rules. I should note, however, that my client defended me like a champion, because his wife and father-in-law were on the contractor's side. That gives you an idea of the kind of people I'm talking about. Outrageous. The poor bricklayers, at least, were good-natured about their complaints:

"But sir, when people see this they're going to say that we don't even know how to lay bricks properly. . . ."

There was one young man among the bricklayers, a rather sullen type, who visited me every Friday for a bit of

bodywork. And what a body he had, girls; Michelangelo's
*David* couldn't hold a candle to him. Prickwise he was fine,
nothing out of this world, mind you, but his stamina and
temperament drove me wild. Every time, just after penetration, he would lick his lips, slide his hand between my legs,
and then push it upward, as if he wanted to break me in two:
"You're going to have to beg me to stop."

Ah, my little angel of innocence. By the third time he
began to get an idea of what I'm made of. But he kept re-
peating his remark anyway.

That's a topic for another disquisition, I know, but I
think it's worth it. And stop rushing me, will you? I can't
take the stress, ladies. This goddamn cast has me completely
on edge as it is.

That little bricklayer, who was a mere sixteen-year-old
(I'm a regular cradle robber—what a thrill), had one weakness: he would beg me to sit on top of him, fully dressed but
with his zipper down and a distended, stiff rod, the kind
that only an adolescent could maintain, jutting out. And his
balls bulging just beneath the surface, like quail eggs tucked
into their little Levi's nest. It was like riding on the outstretched finger of your favorite guardian angel, naughty but
innocent at the same time, and as I obliged him, his baby
face would break into a smile of pure joy. He didn't even let
me take his Jockey shorts off, because he liked to be completely clothed, shoes included, whereas I was fully naked
except for my panties. Everywhere I go I always carry with
me about half a dozen pairs, the high-class hooker kind, the
tiniest little things that nonetheless manage to do a damn

good job of hiding the spurious gifts nature gave me, just in case a particular evening called for some deliberate confusion. And that was exactly the ticket with the bricklayer.

"Don't show me your cunt, I'd rather just imagine it," he said.

He preferred to lie on top of the bedspread, so as not to make a mess of the sheets. I turned the shutters down so that the shadows would help me look more like the woman he wanted me to be.

"You've got a bod like a little girl," he whispered. "Just the way I like it."

And then, as I sat on top of his legs, he asked me, in the faintest of voices,

"First press that massive cunt hard against my cock. That's it. . . . Mmm, nice and hot."

I rubbed it to and fro, ever so slowly. He asked me to stroke his cock with the palm of my hand, without grasping it fully.

"Easy, baby, take it easy. Put a little spit on the head," he implored, and I obliged with my hand. Just as he requested, just as he liked it. Slowly.

"I'm going to stick it in," I said. "Slowly." Without taking off my panties. Stretching the elastic a bit with my fingers.

"That's it. Don't move." With his free hand, he continued to thrust his prick forward.

"A little more spit . . . there. Ooh, that hurts." It burned him.

"Don't move." I let the tips of my fingers lightly skip over his cockshaft.

"Move it a little—ooh, sparks. Move forward a little." The head of his prick was now almost inside my panties, pressing against the elastic of the leg opening.

"Balance it a little. There, like that. Ooh, that's good, man." As if he were talking to some friend. His eyes half shut. Green, as green as emeralds. What eyes.

"Ooh, that's good. What a whore, what a fantastic whore you make." What a thing of beauty that boy was. A real gem.

"Move. Move a little more. Let me put it in." I loosened up a bit for him, rising up on my knees. His hands spreading my tunnel open.

"What a cunt, lady. Oh, that's good. Stick it in, all the way in." I did so, but without relinquishing, without letting him take my panties off.

"Move it, come on. I'm inside now. Move, yeah, like that. Move it more. More. Swallow it up, more, swallow it up. Fuck, fuck, that's good, man, real good. . . ." Now I was moving like a mixer, like a real Moulinex, until the mayonnaise went all the way up to my cerebellum. Then, the little hedonist asked me to run a bath for him, with salts and everything, and he soaped himself up, all over, for a long time, very slowly, until it started getting late and he had to go and meet his girlfriend.

There's Kleenex in the drawer over there, girls. You too, Mr. Policeman, you might want to keep a tissue handy.

What a head I've got. I know. I'm getting to it. I've still got some tape left.

You see, Mr. Policeman, I still have to tell you the story of the baker, which is what I originally intended to tell you about.

All right, I'll spare you the introduction. The setting is more or less the same—remember, the little bungalow in Sanlúcar, with views overlooking the nature sanctuary, just outside the neighborhood where I was building that house. A jewel in a garbage heap, that was the house that this humble servant made for her almost ex-brother-in-law, that sucker for the black kiss, a virtuoso, if you recall. If you ever get the chance to meet him, don't miss the opportunity. It's a small world, after all. All right, here's the story: Rota, as you may know, is just a few steps away from the house of the black kiss—if you ever get stationed on a submarine you must take a stroll through this little military base town. And with a little luck, you just might run into my baker.

He came in a vanilla-colored Citroën van—every day, after I left a note on the doorstep of the house next door. You see, it's such a divine treat to have fresh bread delivered to your door—I mean fresh, still warm, just out of the oven, between nine and nine-thirty in the morning. That was when the baker would come around, sometime between nine and nine-thirty in the morning—so amused, so full of smiles, always so happy, that little baker man, who would chirp "Good morning" as if he didn't have a care in the world.

"What will it be today?" he would ask me every day, even though he didn't really have to since I always ordered the same thing.

One breakfast roll; a medium-sized baguette for lunchtime (whatever was left over was good for making toast to accompany my afternoon coffee); and little ladyfingers for after dinner. Always the same. But it was clear that he was not interested in taking liberties.

Of course, ever since the day I first saw him, I was desperate for him to take all the little liberties that might cross his macho mind. All of us clients must have been thinking the same thing. Yes, ladies—you, who are such movie buffs, remember what a buck that Burt Lancaster was when he was young? Well, that's what this guy was, only minus the big hairdo, with a little more spunk, and a set of lips that curled up in the most adorable, flirty manner. Naturally, he caught on to me from the start—I had made my intentions crystal clear. Oh, how obvious it all sounds in the retelling. . . . No words, I don't need words. Specific words, I mean. I said hello, naturally, casual but good and insinuating. I told him that I was thrilled to have him deliver my bread every day— except Sundays, as he reminded me—and I said that it was like a little gift from heaven to be able to start the day with tender, warm bread delivered by a handsome, healthy, smiling young man, without even having to leave the house. I can be quite discreet, as you can see. And don't think that the little blondie got scared off. You should have seen the devilish look on that saintly face . . . speaking of which, can you tell that blonds are my weakness? I bet you, Mr. Policeman, are a radiant blond. Just like the baker man. And I'm not talking about one of those transparent blonds, no — I like them solid, with bronze, sun-kissed skin and a prick the color of crème caramel. Just so we understand each other.

Believe me, ladies, he got hard as soon as I gave his cock the once-over with my evil eye. Quite a stallion, yes sir. One of those men who seem shorter than they really are at first glance. Well-proportioned, consistent, addicted to a single pair of jeans, always immaculate and freshly ironed, frayed in all the right places: to the left of the fly, along the lines of his leg muscles, just above the knee, at the indentation in the middle of his ass.

"Do you plan on staying here long?"

He had a supple, playful voice.

"Five or six months, at least," I said. "I'll have to find something to break the monotony, won't I?"

His mouth broke slowly into a smile, and his thoughts came tumbling from his lips.

"Well, we'll have plenty of chances to talk when I'm not so rushed."

"To talk and anything else you want to do," I said, and anyone could have seen that those were exactly the words he wanted to hear.

We agreed to settle the bread bill every Saturday, to avoid the bother of dealing with exact change every day.

"Three seventy-two," he announced after mentally calculating what I would have to pay him at the end of the week. "That is, if you don't order anything else."

And then I warned him:

"Better prepare yourself."

I never would have guessed he would be such a prude. In certain ways, I mean. There is no understanding young people these days; they are full of surprises at every turn. And the baker is a perfect example. They say that Miss Balcony possesses talents capable of melting anyone's misgivings. But this kid was beyond that, beyond help entirely.

Every day, I would greet him, looking sensational. The first few days I wore a jogging suit, sporty and casual, specifically so that my little darling would know that all he had to do was say the word and I would be at his disposal in any which way he wanted. I showered, gave myself a nice spray of eau de toilette—a light lavender scent, because the last thing I wanted was to suffocate the poor thing with some steamroller perfume. And I always made sure to satisfy a strategically located itch somewhere on my body whenever he was in front of me. We went on like that for a week and the kid did nothing but smile devilishly and carelessly scratch his package, always at the very last moment, just as he was getting into his van to move on with his deliveries. The conversation, incidentally, was nothing out of this world, either.

"I didn't sleep so well last night," I said one day. "I guess I'll have to take a nap today." And he said,

"I wouldn't trade my nap for anything in the world, I can't think of anything better than taking a nap bucknaked." And then I said:

"Well, if you ever find yourself in the neighborhood, I've got a huge bed here." And then he said:

"If I take you up on that, I can't be held responsible for my actions." To which I said,

"I've seen everything in my time, honey." And then he replied,

"That's what you think."

We left it at that, and let me tell you, this humble servant was fit to be tied. So I decided to try lightening up my look a bit, and that first Friday I greeted him in a pair of sporty little culottes, purchased three seasons earlier at one of Ibiza's chicest boutiques, ladies, and on top, a pink blouse with spaghetti straps that showed off my tummy—you know I've got a set of abs on me like nobody's business—don't be vulgar now, ladies, come on. With that, he couldn't help but notice the effect.

"You've still got a hot bod, you know that?"

Yes, girls, I know, I could have done without the "still" but he said it with such intensity that it came out sounding like a compliment. Definitely a compliment. I murmured my thanks as gratefully as if the Queen had just knighted me. I focused my gaze directly onto the prize. Very slowly I scratched myself in a most strategic location, batting my eyelashes, as if I couldn't believe what I was seeing. I acted as though swallowing my saliva took the most Herculean effort. And then I attacked. Verbally, of course.

"You know, I'm dying to ask you something."

"What?"

"That enormous bulge outlined beneath your fly—is it everything I think it is?"

"Everything. And more."

"More? Impossible."

He hiked his pants up a little and with his two hands firmly cupped the turgid package encased in his jeans. A package that would have left you cross-eyed for life, ladies, believe me. My eyes haven't been the same since.

"You can't even imagine what this gets like when it's hard," he said.

"I'd love to see it."

"I know. You think I can't tell?"

That last bit came out in a different tone of voice, and it changed the rhythm of our banter entirely. It was as if he had lost control of himself and gotten carried away with that momentarily perverse pleasure. All of a sudden it turned into a different kind of conversation entirely, and I hope you can appreciate this subtle distinction. Now it was a battle of wits.

"You wouldn't dare, I can tell that."

"I don't like to be left cold."

"I'm sure. It's probably not what it seems. Appearances can be so deceiving in this sort of thing."

He smiled. Then he reached into the van and removed a baguette, the same kind that he sold to me every day, the same kind I ate every day at lunchtime. With his free hand he clutched his own bulky package.

"The mold for this is right here," he said, manhandling the baguette in such a way that I could feel my cunt beginning to cry out. I tried to keep my voice from trembling.

"I bet yours is smaller."

"That's what you think."

"Well, you won't show it to me, isn't that proof enough?"

"It's better inside than out."

"Oh, that's what I was afraid of."

"What?" he asked, ever so calmly. Nothing could ruffle that motherfucker.

"Just what you said. That it's better inside your pants than out. Maybe that's the problem, that you don't know what to do with it."

"Don't worry about that. These things are fast learners."

At this point I was ready to have a fit. But yoga, ladies, came to my aid once again.

"You've already got someplace to put it, then?" I asked, disdainfully. "Aside from your jeans, I mean."

"No."

"You're not married, are you?"

"No."

"Girlfriend?"

"Yeah."

"Well, what? Doesn't your girlfriend have a cunt? Can't she suck it off for you?"

"Well, no. Not yet."

At that moment, I still didn't realize what he was trying to say to me. I was agitated. My reflexes were off. Such a combative tug-of-war at nine-thirty in the morning would have worn out the cleverest among us, girlfriends. It was as if I had suddenly lost my ability to walk.

With a flourish, he flung open the back door of the van. Total aplomb. And smiling, too. He sat down inside, so that only his feet dangled out. And then he called out to me:

"Come here."

He was massaging his package now.

"Come closer. I want to tell you a secret." With two fingers he grabbed his thickened prick. "I think you're a strange little bird."

At first glance, I could see that it wasn't completely hard. Of course, I could have cared less; I was on the verge of a coronary by now.

He began to caress my thighs, and then he slid his hand under the opening of my shorts and with his index finger began to look for my little pleasure hole. Athletic wear has a way of making things so much easier.

"You're on fire."

"But that little sausage hasn't grown an inch, has it?" It was starting to piss me off a little.

"Don't get angry. That's the way she is, you know? I know it might seem strange, but I already told you she's not typical. But that has its advantages, don't you think?"

"What? What advantages? Tell me. Oh yes, don't stop." I was ready to faint from that finger tickling me like that. "Tell me. What could you possibly mean by that?"

"You're on fire. You're ready to explode, baby."

"Don't stop. Oh, what pleasure, my little man. Keep going."

"It's a shame, isn't it? He just doesn't want it, you know? You like it, don't you? Tell me how much you like it."

"I like it, sweetheart. I love it. You're driving me mad, I'm going to die right here. Like that, do it like that. Soft and tender. Oh, what joy. What do you mean he doesn't want it?"

"My prick doesn't want it. He just doesn't."

"Why not?"

"That's the way he is. Weird. He wants to belong to the woman I marry, that's all."

That's what he said.

Just to pee—not an errant drip anywhere else.

The tough part was that I was ready to roll. I couldn't think straight; I couldn't even laugh. I gripped his wrist and between gasps I begged him to give it to me with his arm, all the way down to the elbow.

"Give me the whole thing, baby, down to your elbow, your armpit," I pleaded, as he implored,

"Wait, just wait a little." Then he buried his face in my stomach. He was on fire. His tongue, his saliva were hot as he licked my navel frantically.

"Come, come—I want you to come, I want your milk to overflow." And all I could do was press my body against his wrist and arm and beg,

"More, please, a little more, a little more, please." Oh, his hands were like barrels.

"Tell me when you're going to come, tell me," he said, and I kept saying,

"Don't stop, whatever you do, don't stop, keep going, keep going, deeper, higher, keep going." And as he licked my stomach, bathing me in a saliva that grew thicker and hotter all the time, he said,

"Oh, what a shame, baby, what a shame. . . . Don't move now, don't get scared, you'll see, you'll see how good it's going to be, you're going to love it, don't move now, stay cool, stay cool now, hold on a little, now you're going to see how good it is with a baguette. . . . " Crusty, that lightly burnt, soft baguette of his.

"That's it baby, that's it, it's just like my prick. There now, slowly, carefully, we don't want to break it now . . . there, there." And there I was, agitated and incredulous, desperately trying to hold back the orgasm, feeling that monstrous thing as it slowly entered me, and I hung on to the baker's wrist, that giant hand that so very slowly, so very wisely continued pushing the 45-centimeter baguette, still crusty and hot, farther inside me.

"There, baby, all the way in, all the way up, I want you to come. Tell me when you come, tell me," he said, and I wasn't aware of anything anymore, I was like a sleepwalker in ecstasy. I didn't even realize when or how that adorable creature took off my shorts, until finally I fell backward onto the immense basket of bread, my legs raised up high, with that boy nibbling away at my navel, with his hand softly pushing in and pulling out the baguette that was just like his prick, a perfect copy, exactly like that prick that insisted on being claimed only by the woman who would marry its owner. Strange, ancient, secret—"But that has its advantages, don't you think?" Oh, yes. Such restraint, such control always has its advantages.

"I want you to come, to come," he said to me, panting, moaning, prolonging the pleasure as if it held the key to life itself, as if all his honor were wrapped up in it, as he clung to my waist like a child lost in an amusement park, happy, so happy when I finally said "I'm coming, I'm coming, I'm coming," happy to have given me such happiness.

We did that every Friday. I'm done now. Finished. Every Friday. And every Saturday we settled accounts: four euros and seventeen centimes, forty-five centimes more than we had assessed at the beginning, for that additional baguette every Friday morning.

# II

*Where Herr Betty Honey complains
of Miss Balcony's vices and defends
the beauty of love, and at the same
time proves that the police can
be useful for more than
just hunting down queers*

Mr. Policeman: "Hello, Hello Dolly"—what a lovely song. I want that song playing in the background the whole time. My colleague Miss Balcony has said everything she had to say straight up, without the least bit of flair, whereas I am a sucker for music. A contemporary, international song, nothing folkloric or middlebrow. Streisand singing off in the distance as I tell you everything I have to tell.

It's not that I'm trying to make anyone look bad, mind you. To each his own, I say, and in my case, well, I have my own standards and my own values. I'm sure that you gringos, when you enacted that tedious law against certain modes of behavior that bring such pleasure and release to man, had decided that such behavior is nothing but the result of vice and evil seed, but I promise you one thing: ask around and you will find that those acts are acts of love, abundant love.

Those things that you condemn, those things that you so
politely and discreetly call oral and anal sex, are often bathed
in love. [Miss Balcony's voice, off in the distance: "Yeah, baby,
like a merengue bathed in honey!"] Oh, they are awash in
emotion, tenderness, surrender, and affection. I think you may
have a few misguided notions about us, and I can understand
why: the loudest voices always seem to cause the greatest fuss,
and often give off an image that I wouldn't exactly call bad —
because I'm certainly not one to condemn my sisters — but so
very often our image is disguised by frivolity and vice, while
the real truth about us never comes out. [Miss Balcony's
voice: "My God, this lady sounds like a preacherman!"]

I don't care what they say; I just want you to understand me. To understand all of us, because even those of us
who may seem hopelessly obsessive and deviant, in fact, have
a great capacity for love and tenderness. [Miss Balcony's
voice: "Of course she's right: the capacity of my cunt is as
deep as King Solomon's mines."] This is the truth, no matter how hard they try to hide it because it embarrasses them
to come off as sensitive, generous souls. From my perspec-
tive, they're just a bit unaware, and they don't realize the
harm they cause the rest of us. [Miss Balcony's voice, again,
in the distance: "Oh, come on, this is too much. We got
Therese of Lisieux, the country bumpkin saint, with us
today."]

Now, please. I think I have the right to speak without
being interrupted. [Miss Balcony: "Oh, come on, baby, stop
being so pretentious. The way you talk anyone would think
you're as pure as the Virgin Mary, and your cunt as squeaky

clean as a day spa. Why don't you leave the rest of us alone already and just tell the boys your little story."]

Well, it's just that my story will be misunderstood if I don't make it clear that I did what I did for love. Plain and simple. I broke it off with a perfectly wonderful man who loved me, and left him in a state of utter desperation and loneliness, all because I suddenly realized that I was unable to respond with the kind of love he deserved. I'm an honest woman, Mr. Policeman, and proud of it. Nobody can accuse me of pretending to be in love out of selfishness, convenience, habit, or pity.

That's what I said, in all honesty, to Toshiro. My Toshiro was Japanese. [Miss Balcony's voice: "Well, he still is, baby. The other day, before my little misadventure, I saw him on the boulevard, on Recoletos, and he's still as yellow as ever, with those almond eyes of his. What did you think, that he'd suddenly turn into a Hapsburg?"] He was perfectly charming—so delicate, so exquisite, so meticulous. But after six months I realized I wasn't in love with him, a realization that, I am aware, may have come a bit late, for we were together long enough for him to get his hopes up. I allowed him to get much more deeply involved than he should have. With his heart ripped to shreds, I told him I was leaving him. [Miss Balcony's voice: "And your Toshiro, so very practical and Japanese, told you quite directly, 'That's fine, go to hell, honey.' Or 'herr,' as he pronounced it. And therein your nickname, Herr Betty Honey. Admit it."]

Lies, all lies. My name is Bettino, and my nickname is the logical consequence of my sweetness. I am a doctor, with a specialty in dermatology, and I work in a medical collective in the neighborhood of El Pilar, next door to the Vaguada shopping mall. And so, when I broke up with Toshiro, I rented an apartment in the same neighborhood—small, but really cute, very sunny and everything. Anyway, that was how things turned out after that episode.

I won't mention specifics about Toshiro and our relationship, because the memory often grows foggy in matters of unrequited love, and that, to me, would be wrong. [Miss Balcony's voice: "Don't sweat it, baby, we all know Toshiro had a ridiculously small prick. But you can tell us all about his fabulous tongue, that's part of the story too."] That affair is like a dead tree to me now, and to spin carnal tales about it, knowing that no love was lost, would be like spiting the dead tree by showering it with all the green leaves that never blossomed on its branches. [Miss Balcony's voice: "Oh, please!"]

If you don't shut up for once and for all, you bitch, then I will. [Miss Balcony's voice: "That's the way I like it, ma'am: fire, bristle, balls. Let your hair down, baby. Miss Betty Balls. Violence and sex. And I promise from now on to keep my trap shut."]

All right, let's see if you can. With respect to Toshiro, as I said, not a word. Love has me prisoner now, and has rendered me helpless. The past no longer exists. The present is named Eusebio, and I love him. The present is named Eusebio Gutiérrez Ríos and he lives in my building, in the entrance next door. He lives with his brother, his sister-in-law, and his niece Vanessa. The apartment belongs to his

brother, but Eusebio naturally pays him for rent and main-
tenance each month, and though I think he pays too much
I'm tired of telling him already. Eusebio always says that for
now it's fine, though maybe one day he'll take the plunge
and move in with me so that I can take care of him. He needs
someone to take care of him, to protect him. On his account,
and on account of the kind of work he does, I live on tenter-
hooks. For me, the past is no longer dangerous. The present
is what consumes me. The present is called Eusebio and he
is an officer of the law, just like you, Mr. Policeman.

For me it was cupid's arrow, the kind of love that ig-
nites at first sight and forces you to take inventory of your
conscience, of all your defects and virtues so that you can
quickly assess precisely what love can expect of you. [Miss
Balcony's voice: "In other words, instantaneously calculate
the balance of your checking account. Oh, forget I just said
that, honey. . . ."] So that's where we are. I simply cannot
understand why so many of you insist upon denying the
existence and power of love. I cannot understand what is
so fascinating about one-night stands with a random stranger
who happens to cross your path. I don't know what people
see in that. Disappointment. Misfortunes like yours, Balcony, in the best of cases; encounters with those boys who
would follow you on their motorcycles through that hideous,
infamous Daddy's Drag—that empty lot near the univer-
sity, just off the exit to the La Coruña highway, that was
both setting and sanctuary of the greatest excesses known
to faggots of all ages, sizes, and colors during the somber
nights of Franco's dictatorship—forcing you to dive into

roadside pits to avoid getting run over by one of them. They almost killed you once, and they could have easily succeeded, even though they only left you mangled beyond recognition and with your left tibia ripped to shreds. Perversion is simply not worth the trouble, my dear friends. Perversion destroys. Perversion crushes everything in its wake. Love, on the other hand, is all-redeeming.

Love found its way to my heart like a hungry boar when I surprised that boy with the arrogant figure and slow-motion moves as he undressed in his bedroom. It was summertime, and as he entered his room and turned on the light, he glanced over at the building next door, as if looking out for some undesirable soul who was pursuing him. I, in fact, was pursuing him (fortunately, with the bathroom light off), but in no way can I be considered undesirable. I'm not trying to hard-sell myself or anything, Mr. Policeman, but I can sense things, just as one can sense the arrival of spring by the scent of the almond blossoms in the air. And as it happens, I sense that I awaken certain passions in people, and my job is neither to encourage nor to take advantage of them. Those are the facts, my dear friends, even if they fall on deaf ears. [Voice of Miss Balcony: "Deaf ears and blind eyes, darling."]

I continue. I shall not acknowledge this last interjection because, to a certain extent, I brought it on myself. Mea culpa. [Voice of Miss Balcony: "Blame it on your boyfriend, baby!"] I repeat: Mea culpa. As I was saying, he looked at the building across the way to ensure that he wasn't being indiscreet; a simple gesture, but it touched me deeply, be-

cause his brother's apartment is entirely interior—that is,
all the rooms have windows that face out onto the central
patio that our two buildings share, and from my bathroom
I could observe every last bit of that family's private life if I
wanted to, because in point of fact the adult couple in that
family is not exactly a paradigm of modesty, and little Vanessa
is scarcely old enough to even know what modesty is. And
that was why it was so moving to me, that such a beautiful
boy would be so modest, when in reality nobody with an
ounce of sensitivity would ever have balked at the vision of
him exhibiting the gifts that Mother Nature so wisely gave
him. What a contrast he made with the obscene disregard
of his brother and sister-in-law. Eusebio's brother is a bus
driver on the M3 line, which starts at the Plaza de Callao
and terminates in the neighborhood of El Pilar, two hops
from where we all live. In general he works the morning shift
and as such obliges his wife to join him in the most ferocious,
violent, interminable siestas that—in summertime, especially—are highly unadvisable viewing for a neighbor such
as myself. Eusebio's brother is a man of still-forgivable age
but with a vulgar physique: rather truncated in stature,
a Mohammed-like face, boorish mannerisms, a rural, noisy
voice, happy in his own way, and covered in unrefined
muscles from the waist up, and unrestrained nerves from
the waist down. His fountain of perdition, one might say, is
a bit overly pronounced. Nothing but the most primitive
upbringing could possibly explain, as far as I can see it, the
mad attraction his wife feels for him. She, on the other hand,
is a girl of somewhat delicate appearance—she manages to

achieve a certain personal style when she gets dressed up
to walk little Vanessa through the park next to the Vaguada
shopping mall but in the privacy of their boudoir she turns
into a veritable nymphomaniac straight out of the jungle. It
almost disgusts me, I can't help it. The bus driver takes all
of five seconds to rip off his clothes, as if Phidias the Greek
were telling him to make it as quickly as possible. Educa-
tion and culture, Mr. Policeman, are the haven of the spirit.
And then, without even waiting for his poor wife to take off
her apron, he forces her to suck him off. It is an act of truly
nauseating brutality, but once he casts his spell on her, she
is a woman transformed. That woman has such dental in-
continence that her husband instantly starts shrieking like
a stuck pig and then she has to separate his butt cheeks with
her two hands as he begs her to make crochet out of his
sphincter—to compensate, I suppose.

And so the raging bull has a splendid time of it while
his wife works him over like a slave woman. It's disgusting
to see how that purple garden hose of his grows and grows
in the lips of a poor housewife with no other choice than to
give her owner and master his pleasure. Whenever I watch
this, I am frankly petrified. I cannot even move, or look away
from the window. I tighten my thighs against the bath tiles
like a bitch in heat. I have to douse myself with a can of spray
deodorant just to calm down my back door during this tem-
porary paralysis. It's hell, Mr. Policeman, because I am sure
that there is no love lost between them. There is no love in
that animal couple's delirium and carnal gluttony, or in the
sickly throbs of that man who I swear looks virtually ill from

pleasure, or in the lascivious devotion of that woman. When she separates her mouth for a moment from the cylindrical source of her disgrace, trembling like a lady bullfighter brought to her knees, and grabbing her husband's monstrous cock like a shipwreck victim clings to a life preserver, I can tell that she will spend the rest of her life exactly like that. I don't doubt this for a second. You have to see it for yourself to understand it, I suppose. But it must be some kind of compensation for a lifetime of submission and strolls through the Vaguada mall. Her only revenge on life. It drives her nuts. She hikes her skirt up to her tonsils. The way she manages to squat down with her legs spread wide open, my God, she deserves to be put on a television show, just for the performance. Her panties, of course, get destroyed in the process; that poor woman must require such a huge underwear budget that I'm not surprised they charge my Eusebio so much for his room. She sticks her finger in up to her wedding band, she smears him with it, twists it every which way. All this, mind you, without letting that miraculous bazooka out of her mouth, without giving her husband a moment of rest. It's almost as if she were exercising all the pent-up rage she feels for the bus driver and Vanessa and the whole neighborhood of El Pilar and the Vaguada mall — exercising it in the most sibylline fashion: by giving her husband a pleasure so intense that it becomes pain. And demanding a violent, residual, indecent kind of pleasure in return. Because then she rests on her husband's calves, pressing her red-hot meat against them, sliding farther and farther down toward his feet and gripping his ankles, so that the lips of her vagina can finally be penetrated by his hairy, deformed, filth-encrusted toes, decorated with callouses, corns, and the blackened, warped toenails of a pair of feet hardened and bloated in the daily struggle against brake and clutch. Half his foot disappears, as if by magic, into the cunt of that delicate creature as she convulses with happiness and her man trembles, still overcome with lust at the beatific hour of the siesta, crying out "filthy bitch" at the top of his lungs. Scandalous, I tell you. It must be nothing less than a scandal for the entire apartment building, the entire neighborhood, even. And nobody has uttered a peep in protest. Nobody, I tell you. Myself included, of course, God help me. Love cannot possibly dwell amid that warped delirium of theirs, and I know this because love is a warm, welcoming cascade that is all-embracing and all-pacifying. And as if that weren't enough, these two end their sex sessions by screaming their vows of mutual love to one another. But they are fooling themselves. They are merely hypnotizing each other for as long as it takes to digest their lunch. After the first round the two of them flop down on their double bed, and I must say, it's a bit frightening to see that giant cock all black-and-blue as if threatened by gangrene. By the look of it, one could easily say that his cock was badly in need of intensive care. Or at least some prolonged bed rest. But it is a rest that never comes, because that wife of his does not give up so easily. Before he is allowed to surrender to sleep, she jumps up from the bed, begins hunting in the built-in closet, and pulls out the National Police's winter jacket — my Eusebio explained to me one day that since this is the only closet in the house, he stores his out-of-season uniforms there. Then she extracts a pair of army-issue combat boots and white gloves that are part of the National Police dress uniform. She puts her hero in this getup and then she dons a silk shawl and a bedsheet in a quick improvisation of an army-tramp number for herself. Once I actually heard her say, in a raspy, greasy, whorehouse voice,

"Come on, let's playact what you did with that little slut who was so hooked on you when you were in the army." And that was when I understood that sick, obscene game they often play for the remainder of the siesta—he, a caricature in a brown jacket that barely covers his indiscretions, swimming grotesquely in the gigantic boots, stuffing the white gloves full as if he were about to take his first communion, and tripping all around his bedroom in his role as clumsy recruit; she, meanwhile, preening and posing like a bad actress in a bad movie, playing a tart who pursues her prey like syphilis pursues sailors from port to port. She always playacts the same scene of never being able to fully seduce him, sweet-talk him, or get him horny quickly or consistently enough. She does this until he responds, playing his role of inexperienced, nervous young man who then suddenly rises up and pounces upon her, knocking her down, pressing her arms and legs against the floor and attacking her with his manliness as forcefully as one would fire a Mirage. And despite the fierce resistance of his whorish companion, who stops at nothing, biting hard and very authentically into his flesh, he nevertheless continues on with the rape scene until she cries out "My period, I have my period," and then obe-

diently allows him to turn her around, her ass cheeks bulging in perfect twin curves, her face pressed against the par-
quet floor. Then he impales her cleanly from behind amid a
chorus of spasms and moans, in one long, muscular pump-
ing maneuver that ends just as my strength fails me and, in
a puddle up to my heels, I lose consciousness.

Believe me, Mr. Policeman, the proletariat in this country will stop at nothing. As those of us who are members of
the privileged class would say, "What on earth have we come
to?" [Miss Balcony's voice: "You, baby, you better come
with me to the eye doctor, you bourgeois sonofabitch, working that visual with such bad lighting."] As you can see, people
will use any excuse to call you a bourgeois sonofabitch, when
all I'm trying to do is point out that people are what they
are, and I don't think that implies any disdain or crime on
my part. My Eusebio's brother and sister-in-law should
focus a little more on Vanessa and a little less on their perverted sex games; as it is they act as though life is one big
game. If there was any real love in that relationship, Vanessa
would be the very center of their existence, because true love
needs to perpetuate itself and children fulfill that need. That
is how I see things, Mr. Policeman, I am traditional and
prudent when it comes to the basic pillars of life, and I hope
my story helps law enforcers like yourself to reconsider your
opinion of us. Well, *some* of us, naturally, because I certainly
don't approve of sinners who take advantage of the virtue
and sacrifice of those who are in the right.

But wait—there's more I want to say. If one day Eusebio
finally decides to move in with me, we will do everything in

our power to adopt Vanessa. We've spoken about it at length already, and we are prepared to do whatever it takes. Personally, I think any judge would award us custody after watching that child's parents at siesta time from my bathroom window. Eusebio and I think it would be an open-and-shut case. [Miss Balcony's voice: "You would know, baby, you're an expert at the open-and-shut game. For God's sake, are you kidding . . . ?"] Envy has a way of making people think that the more they talk, the better they come off; they have a saying for that in my hometown. I should note that Eusebio is the child's godfather, which entails certain responsibilities, and the courts are very understanding in this type of situation; the law has evolved quite a bit. The courts' primary concern is the child's welfare and proper upbringing. And for me, Mr. Policeman, it would be such a dream come true. Vanessa would be my everything. She's such a beautiful, clever little girl. She was named Vanessa in honor of Manolo Escobar's daughter, and in fact my Eusebio was the one who named her—his niece, I mean; not Manolo Escobar's daughter, obviously. Some people disagree, but I know this is true, and it is such a humble, Christian name.

For Vanessa, Eusebio and I would gladly sacrifice our private life. Now, it is true that the two of us drive one another wild whenever we're together—it would be absurd to deny that—but with Vanessa in our care things would have to change. Radically change. I haven't spoken about this with my Eusebio, but I am sure that he would agree with me. When the time comes, I know that he will be the first one to say "Let's give it a rest, baby, let's try and control

ourselves and behave appropriately for the sake of the child."
Because a child of that age cannot help but sense what her
parents are doing behind closed doors—and that can't help
but have some kind of effect on her psyche. And I'll tell you
another thing: during those siestas, which always last at least
three hours, Vanessa doesn't utter a peep, which can only
mean one of two things. Either she is irreparably traumatized by the situation or else her parents are slipping some
drug in her Fanta at lunchtime. Given that this matter involves his own blood brother and sister-in-law, Eusebio
swears this isn't true, that the little girl has always slept like
a baby and in fact has shown no signs of trouble at all.

She could be all the trouble she wants with me. I
wouldn't deny her anything. Just consider the day of her
first communion: her uncle wanted nothing more than to
give her one of those huge, instant Polaroid cameras as a
gift. Of course it was prohibitively expensive—not the camera itself, but all the paraphernalia that came with it. Don't
try to tell me otherwise—that fabulous little gadget is a
money hog. But darlings, Eusebio had his heart set on giving her that camera, and the poor thing was desperately low
on funds, so I gave him the money—and I was overjoyed to
do it, don't get me wrong, I was thrilled to be able to make
both uncle and niece happy. But that doesn't change the fact
that the little contraption is a money vacuum. And everyone, I mean everyone in that family, has gotten hooked on
the camera.

I did not attend the first communion, but that is perfectly understandable, I think. Eusebio, however, did tell

me that our gift was an instant hit, and he was careful to make sure that the family didn't use up all the film cartridges he had given Vanessa. You see, Eusebio wanted to take some photos of the little girl in a quieter moment, in the apartment, as a special memento of the happiest day of her life. I got to watch him take those photographs. I watched them from my bathroom window, just by chance, really—it's not as if I was spying on them or anything. It happened much like the first time I saw Eusebio undressing in his bedroom, the day that infatuation hit me and I realized that I had fallen in love with him like a schoolgirl, after he had looked around to make sure the coast was clear and then stood there bucknaked, with that perfect, hard body of his, that delicious rod, so discreet, so unintimidating . . . oh, and the endearing way he leaned against the wall, totally nude, like a martyr about to be shot through with arrows, until he was no longer able to control his penis, which grew little by little until it was vibrant and pulsating with life. And then he masturbated, slowly and ceremoniously, knowing (finally, after a long time, he confessed it to me) that I was the sole spectator of his masterpiece, a masturbation the likes of which I had never seen before. And to think I had thought the shadows had kept me hidden from view; I was sure he couldn't see me, though of course I secretly dreamt and prayed that he could. Well, it was exactly like that the day he took the Polaroids of Vanessa. He says he could see me across the way, even though I'd made sure the light was off in my bathroom.

Vanessa was in her crisp white dress with the great big satin sash, wide lace appliqués, and tulle veil. The bus driver

had spent a small fortune on his daughter's first communion dress, something I can't help but admire him for. Eusebio
asked her to sit at the edge of the bed and clasp her hands
piously against her chest; that was the first photograph.
Then, he told her to take off the veil and she did, with dif-
ficulty but smiling all the time, just as Eusebio had instructed her. And the camera once again achieved that
miracle of producing a photograph in thirty seconds. Then
Eusebio snapped the camera just as Vanessa took off the
sash—she came out looking just like a cabaret singer. The
next photo was taken in profile with her back exposed,
the dress unbuttoned down to the waist. She faces the camera with a sly look in her eyes, just as her adoring uncle and
godfather asked her to, and yet her face is utterly angelic. I
shocked myself then, for I suddenly found myself getting
aroused. It had to be the optical effect. Then my Eusebio
suddenly began to show some very threatening bulges beneath the fly of the trousers he reserves for special occasions,
though I imagined that was just a question of posture—
everyone knows how photographers always choreograph
their moves just so. Anyway, Vanessa removed her arms
from the sleeves of the dress, which now dangled from her
waist, and Eusebio asked her to arrange the neckline just
beneath her little breasts, and then he snapped the photo.
After that he took another very artistic shot, a pose that
required quite a bit of maneuvering and explanation on his
part: the dress was already resting on the floor, at Vanessa's
feet, and the girl had pulled the neckline of the dress down
to her belly button, and from the other end she pulled up

the skirt high enough to see the edges of her panties. Eusebio repeated that photo, he said, just to be sure. Finally, of course, Vanessa ended up in nothing but her panties, with her long hair cascading down her shoulders, and that innocent look in her eyes, her face tired from such a hectic, emotional day. And so to finish up and give the poor thing rest, Uncle Eusebio asked her for one final pose on the edge of the bed with her legs dangling down, thighs separated (to help the circulation), and with her arms outstretched and her palms facing upward, so that in the photo it would look as if she were waiting for Jesus' warm embrace.

A judge would have to be blind not to see it: Eusebio and I adore each other and our love consists of both power and fantasy, excitement and security, infatuation and ecstasy, delirium and peace. With us, Vanessa would have a home with white walls, transparent organdy curtains, and open doors—doors behind which no unmentionable secrets would lurk. I know myself and can only speak for myself, of course. It might be a bit tougher for Eusebio, because we all know that men have other needs, their own way of seeing things, another kind of understanding of and appreciation for life, and they do have a harder time restraining themselves, that is true. But love has the power to break those chains and withstand tempests and anyway, Mr. Policeman, we've already discussed it. On many occasions I have asked him to join me in making the sacrifice to control our instincts, because I feel that that is how we can prepare ourselves and find the strength for the moment when we must renounce those pleasures, when Vanessa comes to live with us.

"When we have Vanessa," he says, in his self-involved way, "everything will change."

As you can see, despite all my efforts and attempts at reasoning, it is an uphill battle, getting him to control himself. And I must admit that things have worsened since the day of little Vanessa's first communion, since that first afternoon he got off work and appeared at my apartment, in civilian clothes, carrying a duffel bag that contained the little girl's veil and satin sash. I threw myself in his arms—I just love to feel myself sheltered in the biceps of law and order; oh, just thinking of it gets me dilated. Then, with the authority vested in him by his profession, he took me into the bedroom, tickling and touching me in the hallway, though in a more calculated manner than usual.

"I'm going to ask you for a favor," he whispered in my ear as he instructed me to remain on my feet next to the bed. "I want you to dress up for me as you did on the happiest day of your life." And I was simply unable to disobey him in good conscience; indeed, I have nothing better to offer him than the demands of my body and the obedience of my spirit. And in any event, it would have been quite inappropriate to confess that the happiest day of my life was the day I became a real woman, when I first straddled the *Orlando Furioso* of a young dockworker from Cartagena, Spain. Naturally, though, I am no fool and I understood that he was referring to my own first communion—and if you don't believe me, he then gave me the tulle veil and satin sash that he had stolen from his family's armoire, witness of such tremendous candor and lust.

"I'm going to the bathroom for a second," he whispered, in the compact voice of someone who knows he's walking on solid ground. I knew what he was asking me, and so when he returned to the bedroom with his trousers undone and his eyes lit up with lust, I made sure to be all dressed up for him. Rapid-fire, I had taken off my clothes, hiding them beneath the mattress, and I bundled up my body in the white moiré bedspread that my very Catholic sister had given me years before. Who would have imagined that it would be put to such good use now? With the satin sash I improvised a radiant first communion dress, a grand dress for our times, not like the kind they make now, so somber and insipid. The veil was a bit flimsy, to tell the truth, but it did add a saucy little touch to the ensemble. I had time to glance at myself in the mirror, and even I found myself a bit overly arousing, and so I knew I had to focus on affecting that hopeful, innocent look all little girls have on the day of their first communion. The effect, of course, was explosive. The expression on Eusebio's face changed completely; he suddenly looked like a desperate young satyr. It was so touching. He kneeled at my feet like a clairvoyant, grabbed the edge of my improvised moiré dress, and with a voice filled with emotion, said,

"You are an angel, my darling." I *was* an angel with my hands clasped across my chest and my eyes turned upward like a Murillo Virgin Mary, and as he buried his face beneath my voluminous underskirts, he began to lick my ankles as if they were scented with mint. He licked my feet as if they were paradise itself, and he licked my carefully shaved calves, as smooth as the firmament on an early-summer night, and he licked my knees, which trembled like tender peaches. He bathed them in his soft, warm saliva, and with the insides of his lips he caressed them as if they were frightened puppies, rubbing them delicately with his undulating gums, and nipping at them as if they were crunchy bits of toast. I was an angel, licked over and over again by love, by the juicy mouth of that man whose face was the repository of all masculine beauty, with those even temples, that strong, well-proportioned nose, that auburn mustache, so silky to the touch, that generous mouth, pronounced features, smooth cheeks, and firm chin, with a dimple reserved for a select few mortals. I was an angel with thighs assaulted by so many kisses, abused by sinister words, tormented by zealous, lascivious sucking, frightened by the desperate gasps of a national policeman obsessed with drinking the crystalline waters that flowed forth from the heart of innocence and light. From the thighs of the angels.

It's been like this for some time now. Every afternoon he can get off, he comes up to my apartment and asks me for the same thing. I spill the nectar of angels upon his abundant, strong hair, and then I wash his hair with a very exclusive Suave shampoo. He, too, spills the thick, bright white nectar of his devotion, with no consideration at all, onto my carpet, which is hopelessly beyond repair at this point. Those white stains, Mr. Policeman, are the dry leaves of love. The problem is that now I'm worried about debt, because any day now we're going to have to move, to a bigger apartment, I mean. As soon as he takes the plunge to come and live with me and we apply for custody of Vanessa, we will need more room.

"But when we have Vanessa with us," he says, all devilish, to calm me down, "we'll have a real angel in the house."

Isn't that so sweet, Mr. Policeman? Those are the blessings of love. Perversion takes you nowhere. They should tell that to poor little Vanessa, with those filthy parents of hers mired in the mud of their endless, lust-filled siestas. Ask her, and she'll tell you how much she prefers her uncle over them. Eusebio takes care of her. Eusebio takes photographs of her. Lots of photographs. In her bedroom, in the shower, in the pool, on the grass, on sleds. . . . The dear thing has an entire album already, and on the first page she herself wrote an inscription that reads, "Vanessa in Wonderland." [Voice of Miss Balcony: "Swine."] Mr. Policeman, the delights and subtleties of love are reserved only for a select few mouths, and you know what I think: if you've got the itch, scratch it. And if it doesn't go away, come around to the doctor — there are tonics for that sort of thing. [Voice of Miss Balcony: "For God's sake, Mr. Policeman, don't even think of it. This is a dermatologist who prescribes prescription lotions for beauty marks. Take her drugs and your wrinkles will turn into Kaposi's sarcoma."] Oh, you really are a snake. . . . Oh, what a shame. The tape is ending.

# III

*Where Colette la Coco, a well-traveled
executive of many tongues, warns
against the headaches and histrionics
caused by language, and offers a potent
example to illustrate her theory that
words are quite unnecessary in
the pursuit of revelry*

Ladies, the fish dies by the mouth. Well, by language, to be exact. What a waste, my God, so much hot air. That's the problem with languages these days: they are so ostentatious, so excessive, so utterly anachronistic and impractical. Far from ideal in this age of synthesis and economy. [Voice of Miss Balcony: "Verbal synthesis—my God, that's verbal anorexia for a queer."]

I will not stand for interruptions. Consider that a warning.

As I was saying, contemporary communications technology is aimed at precision. Exactitude. We live in the kingdom of precision, of verbal economy. Modern man's ear accepts neither excess nor digression in any sense. You have to make your point succinctly and with as few words as possible. That is the hegemony of semantics. And before

Miss Cleverness here sticks her foot in her mouth, I warn you: the art of semantics is not some queer sex game. Semantics is the very essential science of language in the contemporary world.

A bit heavy on the theory, I realize this. Professional musings, ladies, that's all. It is theory, yes, but a noble one. And anyway, I'll be blunt, so don't worry: Miss Balcony and Herr Betty Honey have been far too emphatic, too full of sincerity, and too ornate in their storytelling. Too many accessories. Adjectives. Adverbs. Too many introductions and conclusions. Too much verbal passion. You have been perfectly dizzying, my friends. The experts claim that modern narrative is, by nature, "telegraphic," and all you have to do is take a look at those American TV shows to see what they mean. Telegraphic, meaning that everything happens in a split second, two words and its over. Not like those tedious series the British make. British television still operates on the lesbianic premise of nineteenth-century dialogue, a major bore that they describe as the "meticulous" or "wordy" approach.

Nowadays, girlfriends, language tends toward compression, so as to be universal. This is the sign of the times; there's nothing you can do about it. I understand that it might be terribly difficult to adapt to this reality, but you have to make a little effort. You all have a weakness for grandiloquent diarrhea of the mouth. In everything. At all hours. With everyone. And this cannot continue. You have to be less racist, for example. Racism is so out of style. Take astringent to your vocal cords, if you must. Racial language, flowery language, exclamatory and onomatopoeic language

can sabotage everything. Everything. That's the way the
world is now, and no, they don't make men like they used
to either.

That is precisely the point I wanted to make. But as
it happens, I have such a compartmentalized mind, the
mind of a successful modern executive, with a clear, well-
structured input—and when I say "input," ladies, I'm not
referring to a spray for your cunt. An impeccable input is
essential for arriving at an informative body of work without a wrinkle or weak point anywhere. We are slaves to technology, what can we do about it? But anyway, the point I
want to make is this: there are scarcely any macho men left
in this great big world of God. Take it from Colette la Coco,
she's got this world very well-traveled.

And there aren't any macho men left in America, either,
Mr. Policeman from Georgia. At least not any genuine, in-
side-out macho men. In America least of all, in fact. Just take
a look around.

Naturally, the phenomenon has an explanation. And
as I intimated, I feel that one must look to language for the
answer. To the mad art of *logos*, my dears. We queers are
just mad about talking, at all times, to anyone and everyone, even during the most intimate moments. And naturally,
ladies, the men of Planet Earth (oh, what I wouldn't do to
meet a man from some other galaxy), from the North to the
South Pole, from East to West, are not made of stone. Let's
see if you can understand what I'm getting at.

Baby dolls, this is what happens: a man arrives in your
life, you offer him your home, you serve him a drink. "Make

yourself comfortable, baby," you say, "I'll be back in a
minute." And you come right back out in a perfect little
number for the occasion, sexy and uninhibited, with your
tall crème de menthe cocktail, and then suddenly, horrified,
you say, "My goodness, excuse me, we have to put on some
music, something soft," your favorite album, Sinatra singing some old songs in that velvet voice of his. And without
looking at him you start to dance, slow and solitary, a dance
that is missing one thing—him. But no, he shouldn't get up
quite yet, you say, get comfortable first, and you draw the
curtains to create a shadowy, conspiratorial atmosphere so
that the air itself will relax a bit too. And then you settle in
next to your beau, wet your lips with the cocktail, and you
feel alive, excited, provocative, aroused, and you snuggle up
next to him. Then you place your hand—a bit nervously—
on his knee and slowly graze it with your well-manicured
nails, and you purr like an Angora kitten and murmur that
you don't know if you can take it much longer. And then, not
very elegantly, things being the way they are, he tells you,

   "Put in the video, baby." And you purr a little more
even though you know it isn't going to do you much good
because he's in control, as usual, because he gets horny much
faster with that scandalously pornographic movie that an
old truck-driver boyfriend gave you, the one who used to
ask you "Come on, put in the video, baby," as if you weren't
satisfying enough for him, as if with you alone he couldn't
reach that level of sexual cardiac arrest. They're all the same.
You always knew it, and you still do but you try to put it
behind you, you try to bury those sad thoughts and not

obsess about it. After all, it's only a game, and he likes to play, it's understandable, he's not being a jerk, he's not looking down on you, it's just the way he is, you tell yourself. Men are all the same—it's a question of glands, they love things that are a little out of the ordinary, that's all. And anyway, you just want them to be happy, you want him to be happy, and when he says, "Come on, baby," those are to be interpreted as words of victory, so you do what he asks and you put the video in, pretending to float like a sleepwalker, as if defending your self-esteem with that semiconscious routine, as if you're not quite aware of what you're doing. And so you put it in and walk back over to him. Submissive, aroused, servile, you rest your head against his chest in search of a few crumbs of romance, but he's not quite one for romance and quickly starts to rush you as he says,

"You *know* it drives me crazy when you touch me that way." And fool that you are, you caress him, full of love and with your ass cheeks quivering all the while, and he says, "No, dummy, anyone can do it like that—come on, do it the way only you know how," and he pushes your head between his legs and instead of fighting for your dignity, you lose control, you open his fly with the precision of a surgeon and you extract his member—so thick, so hard, so pumped up. And he says,

"Suck it all down, baby," and so you start to suck and moan, and during the brief intermissions in which you pause to catch your breath, in those ellipses that you have to insert so that he doesn't come too soon, you say,

"Oh, it's so good, so wild, so tasty." You know how to
do it and when to do it. It's a question of experience. On
the television screen, meanwhile, a group of gargantuan Ger-
mans fuck a couple of Amazons with monstrous tits and
cunts like dump trucks.

"What massive cocks," he says. "What a cock that one
has on him." And that doesn't bother you, really, because
you have his in your mouth, and you lick it, you bite it, you
suck at it, it's delectable. But then he says it again:

"Shit, what a stud, that cock doesn't quit, look how that
girl swallows it all. . . . Yeah, swallow it, eat me up, look how
he shoves it in, oh, that motherfucker's enjoying it, look at
it," and he forces you to turn around with your ass in his
face, just like the girl with the big tits in the movie.

"That German giant is fucking the first actress up the
ass, watch them, watch how much she loves it, she's loving
it, just look at the pleasure on that slut's face," he says, and
you want it too, you rush to please him in every way imaginable. You would have loved to suck his cock bathed in
your crème de menthe. But he's already too far gone, he
wants you to come like the blonde in the movie, just like that,
no lubricant or anything.

"I'm going to rip you apart," he says, "I'm going to split
your black rumba dancer's ass in two, until your come spills
out of your ears," and you rock back and forth as you beg
him to do it.

"Give me everything, my black stallion, all of it, my
love, yes, yes, slow like that, darling, oh, how good, oh you
make me feel so good, so tasty, what indulgence this is, so

good, the best, the best in the whole world, my little boy, heaven, this is heaven." And you start to moan with delight like a bitch in maximum heat, real self-promotion. And that's not good, girls, that we can't keep our mouths shut for even a minute, doing everything we can to make him feel that he's in seventh heaven, that the world was made for nothing other than this, that women don't get half as much pleasure through their cunt. What more do you need? All you have to do is watch it, it's so obvious in the German movies, which are the best, after all. You can see how they fuck the girls up the ass and how crazy they go, those bitches, with the plumber all the way up their pipes, all the way in, up to his balls, what pleasure, baby, how tasty, my little black baby, and he always wants to know if it's true, if he gives you that kind of pleasure:

"Baby, tell me you love it, tell me to give it to you like that," and so you give him everything you've got and your tongue is now going wild, all the richest things you've ever dreamed of come to your lips and you get tense, and you writhe around, and you tell yourself that if there were a camera in front of you this would be an Oscar-winning performance, because you give it your all, you give him everything, you do whatever you have to, and he comes, of course he comes, like an orangutan, like the randiest beast on a stud farm, like the supermacho Viking in the movie. But then he remains pensive for a while, of course he does. The majority of these guys are knocked out by this, ladies, take it from me, and so after the little number we put them through, after so many cries of pleasure and satisfaction, they can't help but get a little pensive and reflect on how incredible it is, what luck, what envy, sonofabitches, that's something else, something worth a try, who knows if I'll decide and finally swing the other way, they think. And they try it, ladies, ultimately they all end up trying it, even the most macho hunk in town will turn around and take it up the ass in a heartbeat, and the minute you're not looking he's giving you his ass, girlfriends. They're so disgusting, all of them, but it's our fault for talking so much, shouting it to high heaven, publicizing it like we do.

How awful. How long. Without periods or anything. I contradict myself, I admit it. But when I get going, I can't help it. Silent, my darlings. We are far lovelier when we are silent. We have to start a campaign, in every language: queers of the world, when you take it up the ass, enjoy it, but do so quietly, because if not the studs will catch on and then they'll want it like that too.

Make love, not speeches.

I understand this is difficult. And I understand that it may be easier for me. So much traveling. All year long racing from one airport to the other. Madness. Next week I have to go back to Cairo.

I adore Cairo. I adore the baths at Al Mkasis. Let me tell you about it. I'll try to contain myself. I will dominate my use of language. I'll be terse, to give you the best possible picture of it; it makes more of an impact that way. The baths at Al Mkasis have it all. Specimens to die for. All of them discreetly cover their privates with a little cloth that, in reality, is perfectly useless. What protuberances. What atmosphere. Nubian decoration scheme. Dark, wiry bodies. Flaming, imploring eyes. Gestures. For you to follow them. They all want you to follow them. The problem is deciding on who. That can cause big problems. It requires ability. Real ability. Eliminating possibilities. Sometimes it works, but usually it's useless. My sister Miss Marcuse told me that the best thing to do is shut your eyes and let Troy burn. You don't know Marcuse, she's secretary of the embassy. She's a wild one, always wears panty hose under her socks when she's dressed as a man. She's a diplomat. She says the proof is in the panty hose. Right now she's stationed in Romania, where she's surely causing all sorts of trouble — she gets boxes and boxes of L'eggs panty hose shipped to her via diplomatic pouch. She got nailed in Cairo for six years, at least. That's not to say she nailed too many Egyptians, though. She's likes to play the worldly diva act, though I don't know what good it does her. Not me. I'm much more practical. I picked one right off. One with a big old mustache. What a body. And what a package under his pants. He gave me a signal. He wanted me to go to the far end of the room, a dark corner. Go for it, I said to myself. As soon as I got up he was at my side, grabbed my hand, and said, "Come with me, my friend." Not another word. We walked toward a kind of hallway. Small. Dark. I walked straight to the wall, facing it. No preambles. Wide open. What a cock, ladies. He entered me like a nervous tic — all of a sudden it was olé, Allah. What ecstasy. Emptied himself in about two seconds — what speed. He was even faster than me, and of course everyone knows that all you have to do is touch me

and I come. That's why the bitches that know me call me
Miss Polaroid. Instantaneous. If I had the time, I would
explain: premature ejaculation is a linguistic dysfunction. I
don't have time. After our little encounter, I grew alarmed—
*this is it?* I asked myself, somewhat disappointed. But ladies,
he was only the appetizer. Another man grabbed the opportunity next. Another cock to die for. Another rapid-fire
penetration. In silence. I tightened my butt cheeks. To hold
him back a little. To make it last. Absolutely pointless. He
inundated me in five seconds. And then there was another.
And another. All of them silent. I got up to fifteen; after that,
I couldn't take any more. What pain. How could I get out
of there? I turned around, my eyes accustomed by now to
the darkness. And what I saw, girls, was horrifying. I almost
fainted. There was a line. A long, long line. As if they were
waiting to get into the movies. How was I to escape? The
man next in line grunted something. He was impatient. He
clearly needed to get off, like, *now*. I fondled him a little to
stall things a bit. A scandalous prick. But either he aimed
wrong, or I moved away at the wrong moment, for in the
ensuing fracas I practically broke my leg. What a rush. What
danger. What luck, in the end. Suddenly there was a commotion in the line. Someone was protesting something. I
made it clear that I was scared, and my companion caught
wind of that, and got scared as well. He turned around to
shout something. The commotion grew, and it looked like
it was going to turn into a fight. What happened? Nothing, nothing, said the poor thing. Bad luck. Some discus-
sion, about God only knows what, had gotten a little out

of hand. That was my one chance. And I took it. I raced out
of there as fast as I could. Shitting bricks. And Marcuse, that
sonofabitch, laughing her ass off.

"Bitch, what are you laughing at?" I asked her.

"The fight," she said. What happened? I asked.

"You're not going to believe it," she said, between gasps
of laughter. "One of them tried to cut the line."

As you can see, my darling girlfriends, the lovely story I have
narrated for you on side A illustrates how language only
causes problems. Without language, action becomes synco-
pated, vibrant, terribly fluid. The use of words is always,
no matter what the language or dialect, voluminous and
voracious, taking up space like a fat lady spreading out on
three seats of a public bus, chomping and snapping her teeth
like a piranha. If we really want to make the most of the
select, special, disturbingly alluring merchandise that we
have to offer, then we have to crush the power of the spoken word.

Take Petofi Square, in Budapest. There are these under-
ground public bathrooms that you reach by walking down
a long, narrow staircase, the kind of bathroom that you can
only enter after introducing a two-forint coin into a rather
curious-looking contraption affixed to the lock on the door.
Really, it's guaranteed action for Hungarian queers. As you
can imagine, these bathrooms get some heavy traffic. They
get especially packed in the early hours of the evening, when
the factories close. And everyone is stunning. When it comes

to men, Hungary and the Czech Republic take the cake —
as one conservative queer I know once said, those are the
miracles brought about by all that suffering. And lately, as
if that weren't enough, the men in Hungary have become
quite bold. They will do anything for a good blow job. And
so they pile into the public bathrooms on Petofi Square,
toting their work satchels, well-stocked with the necessary
two-forint coins, to enter — or exit, depending on the pan-
orama they find inside. When I go to Budapest, I become a
regular addict. And the minute I walk in, the people in there
know it. They see the perversion in my eyes and the deca-
dence of the western world in my body language. From there,
it becomes a veritable symphony of zippers. Sometimes I
even wonder if they have it rehearsed — some men going up,
others going down, and everyone pausing just enough to
display his jewels to all interested parties. From there, it
becomes a simple question of nerve and skill. There are, for
example, true masterpieces that simply don't know how to
exhibit themselves, and then they go and start talking, way
too much for my taste. They ask you all these questions, so
impatient to get out of there, and then they inevitably ask
you if you have an apartment to go to. Poor things, it's hopeless for them. The silent wolves horn in on their territory in
no time, surrounding the foreign lady with their big, swollen rods. The foreign lady, who knows full well that conversation has an arsenic-like effect on this type of situation,
starts sucking away at anything that moves. You can't imagine, girlfriends, the taste of real socialist milk — it's exactly
the same every time.

In the aerodynamic airports of Singapore, on the other hand, the cockjuice is total multilingual chaos, which is far worse. I once sucked off a Lebanese man who had a stopover in Singapore, and I ended up with my ears ringing so badly I thought I was going to explode. All through the encounter, the degenerate kept muttering things that sounded like weird, threatening ultimatums. On another occasion, and with great care and attention to detail, I sucked off a mammoth, bearded Dutchman who worked for the sultan of Brunei. But just before coming—a moment he prolonged quite impressively— the beast started singing a polka in Dutch which made me lose my concentration, and I nearly choked; my God, I thought I was going to have to have a tracheotomy. Of course, this was nothing in comparison to what I had to go through with an adorable Korean man, a member of the South Korean boxing team—a veritable statue of exotic, strong features, chiseled muscles, a marble ass, and an uncommonly huge cock. He was very robotic, though I didn't realize this at first, because I was too busy running my tongue, in the most elegant way I knew how, over his pisshole. As I did this, he produced a Korean–English dictionary from somewhere and began to spit out words like a slot machine, words that rhymed and that must have been arousing to him: "prick" . . . "milk" . . . "silk." I ended up with a robot complex from that one—that had me brushing my teeth with Drano and gargling with Vaseline.

Now, the airport in Brussels is something else entirely, as senseless and soulless as the rest of the city. Brussels always has more executives than a whorehouse, but I wouldn't suck off an executive, not even if you put a gun to my head. Let their secretaries suck them off, that's what they're there for. And on top of it the toilets at the Brussels airport are constantly being repaired; I've never seen an airport with bathrooms in such constant, desperate need of remodeling. But once—only once—a miracle did occur, in the form of a thirtysomething Turk traveling to Riyadh. We understood one another from the get-go. In no time at all he ran his full, spongy tongue across his lips, cradled by a killer mustache, and slid his left hand in his pants pocket. Of course, in order to reach a bathroom that wasn't closed for repair, we had to walk something like a mile. Finally we found a stall and locked ourselves in. He lowered his trousers—no underwear; such a turn-on—and just before I lowered my head, in peerless observation of protocol, he very politely introduced himself:

"My name is Tarik," he said, in extremely polished French. Too polished. I tried hard, because that stud's pole deserved it and then some, but the expression on his face did not change one iota. He seemed utterly used to it.

"*Merci,*" he said smoothly. And then, without the least bit of concern for me, he opened the door, even though I was still wiping off the corners of my mouth with the back of my hand. And the place was not empty—far from it. All executives, all suits and ties. And all of them, without exception, greeted him warmly, in French: *Bonjour, Tarik,* they all said. And that was when I realized, dumbfounded, that the only executives who go to Brussels are precisely those who don't have secretaries.

They'd be far better off going to San José, Costa Rica. There, the minute any European-looking executive gets off the plane, half the male population of the country pounces. Marcuse claims that it is a question of hormones, but I am certain that it is actually a language issue. In a country where clubs are called "discotecs" and whores are called "hussies," there can be no possibility of salvation. They say "little papaya" instead of "cunt"—my God, just hearing it puts your teeth on edge. And they all walk around dressed up as if it were the 1960s, clothes glued to the skin. Even the policemen. The policemen wear their clothes so tight you can see the outline of their soul; and anyone with a little imagination can tell which ones are in mortal sin, which are in venial sin, and which are in the grace of God. Whenever I go to Costa Rica I end up with so many "girlfriends" in tight jeans and giant combs in their back pockets, I go straight to Managua to get some action with Sandinistas— real men, if you know what I mean.

In the Acapulco airport, all the studs who walk past you and brush up against your fly tell you they're cliff divers, but you'll wear out your high heels looking for one with a precipice sharp enough to really stick it to you.

In the Lima airport the bathrooms are all filthy, but the customs agents insist on locking you up in the stalls so they can perform body searches. As one of them gives it to you, his arm impaling you all the way up to his elbow, the others rob you of every last bauble you've got, but it's such divine indulgence you could care less. And now that I know the game, I always arrive with about two pounds of costume jewelry and focus strictly on my pleasure.

In the Bogotá airport, when the cleaning staff realizes that you're Spanish, they ask you to send their regards to the ambassador. As you leave, and tell them you've fulfilled their request, that of course the ambassador remembers them fondly, they drag you off to the bathrooms and promise you that you'll never forget them either. And they're not kidding.

In the Panama airport, the police are just like their counterparts in San José, but usually much darker, and as they give it to you in the bathrooms reserved for military personnel, they try to sell you exorbitantly priced postcards of the Panama Canal that "the goddamn gringos want to steal from us." This humble servant now has something on the order of three thousand postcards, and considering how weak and dilated those big black hunks leave me, I'm seriously considering getting involved in some big American business just so that when their ships pass through Panama, they take me on board.

The advantage in Latin America is that everyone speaks to you in Spanish and as they fuck you, listening to their voices is just like hearing the rain fall. And in that sense the misunderstandings and disasters are minimized.

But in all those other cities scattered across God's great big earth, language can most certainly ruin the loveliest of stories.

When you land at the airport in Honolulu, the welcome brigade—model types, all wearing summery, fun flower prints—tries to teach you how to chirp "Aloha" like a parrot and then they ask the women to step to the right and the men to the left, so that a man and a woman in loincloths can place the obligatory lei around your neck. The more cocky queers stand in the middle and sometimes they don't get a lei at all. In defiance, they say they won't go through the ridiculous "Aloha" routine until someone comes around and fries them up a nice little banana. It's called linguistic blackmail, and I think it's an ideal topic for someone who needs to give a speech at a semiotics conference. In Hawaii, unfortunately, if you don't say "Aloha" like a recently sprung starlet you don't get action. And I don't understand it, I don't know how they do it. That "Aloha" bit is like the secret code you need to withdraw money on your Visa card—if you don't know it comme il faut, forget about any kind of perforation. Even the most outrageous, well-endowed, temperamental queers have to give in and jump through the hoop, chirping "Aloha" like demented parrots. Only then do they earn the right to have some native Hawaiian with a cock down to his knees or some surfer with a surfboard-sized prick drop their drawers for them. Incidentally, if you ever get the chance to go to Hawaii, don't miss the showers on Waikiki beach, the ones near the first breakwater. There, my friends, you'll suck everything—down to the last surfboard, I promise you.

Of course, darlings, one doesn't need to move to Hawaii and rent the bungalow next door to Imelda Marcos to suffer the bondage of language. Take Karachi, for example. One might think that in such an incomprehensible place like

Karachi, if you don't speak the language you can just make yourself understood by barking. Not on your life. Of course, to be truthful, I did not have to defend myself with the local folk, but I imagine that's what it would have been like. What a little trip, girlfriends. My Auckland–Amsterdam flight, on a KLM Boeing 727, made a stopover in Singapore to receive passengers coming from Bangkok, Jakarta, and Kuala Lumpur before continuing on through New Delhi and the aforementioned Karachi. During takeoff from Singapore, one of the engines stopped, and after the subsequent emergency landing I had the opportunity to get intimate in an Orchard Road hotel with a young Dutchman who worked as a crane operator in Wellington. I would have had that man's baby, I tell you. As we landed in Karachi, the little plane lost another engine. One night in the middle of nowhere, in a splendid hotel. But I couldn't get a wink of sleep in that humid room with the toilet bowl next to the headboard, so I went out to the pool, to snooze a bit on one of the plastic lounge chairs. And I wasn't the only one with that brilliant idea. That's where I found them: two huge black men from Cape Verde who had boarded my plane along with a group of men from Galicia. They had just been relieved by a crew rotation on the oil field they worked on, owned by a shipping company in Rotterdam, and hadn't gotten any sleep either. It was hot as hell. They had taken off their shirts and unbuttoned their pants. I lay down, not too far from where they were. I made a real effort not to get up. Useless. I had to check them out, good. I had to try. They said hello. They asked me for a cigarette. I approached them. I looked them up and down with devastating intensity. They smiled, and the entire night became nothing more than two sets of brilliant white teeth. I smiled at them, my lips wet and gleaming. Then, almost in unison, they placed their hands on their ammunition. And I, still on terra firme, made my swan dive. I took one of them in my mouth, as far as it would go. It tasted like lobster. I ripped my panties off and the other one stuck his lobster in as far as it would go—and in his case, that meant all the way. What joy. Suddenly, from somewhere inside the hotel, a dog began to bark. One of the black men said to me, in Spanish:

"Don't you worry about a thing." And then *he* began to bark. The two of them barking as they fucked me like crazy. They barked and barked until the motherfucking dog finally cooled off. Then, the two of them came for the third time. And when I finally surrendered to my two macho men, the color of the night sky, we were locked in an embrace with me in the middle. Then, the one who spoke Spanish commanded me, rather ferociously,

"Bark." And I barked, girls. I howled. A perversion of language.

Now, in the airport at the sultanate of Muscat, a stopover for some European flights destined for Southeast Asia, an entire army brigade greets you, armed to the teeth and deathly silent. Then, the minute you bat your eyes at them they lunge at you like a bunch of hungry jackals. This is what I've been told. Naturally, as soon as we touched the tarmac I started batting my eyes like mad. But all I managed was some bedouin who touched my ass with his machine gun, and the look in his eyes told me that nowhere else in the world would I find better ammunition for *that* particular target.

Not even in Kathmandu. The Kathmandu airport is built into a gorge deep in the mountains, so that as you land you're convinced that you're going to die. Then, once you get over the shock, you fall in love with Kathmandu and you relax considerably, especially if you're coming from India. In Nepal you feel as though you could evaporate into thin air, but I had the good fortune of discovering the police station headquarters, located in the most marvelous remains of an old temple. And all I had to do was get into position and they were more than disposed to abolish all law and order in Nepal.

All of that without uttering a word, girls. The abduction of language.

Of course, now that I think about it, the police chief of the State of Georgia, who is listening to me right now, must think that I have nothing to say about the contiguous United States of America. Or at least that this humble servant knows nothing about that part of the world. Well, prepare yourself.

Now, the airport bathrooms in the U.S. don't help matters much. Once inside, everyone starts talking like mad the first chance they get, and the loudspeakers announcing the arrivals and departures are louder in the bathrooms than anywhere else. Opportunities do occasionally present themselves in the bathrooms of certain bus depots, but one of the most frightening experiences I ever endured was, in fact, at the Greyhound station in Los Angeles, on Ninth Avenue. I had seen some people lurking around the bathrooms near the platforms at the far end of the station, among them: a couple of spectacular black men; a scrawny evangelical minister type; a Hispanic teenager, gorgeous; a pumped-up queer with a full manicure, straight out of Beverly Hills, who looked utterly convinced that she had achieved a perfect proletarian look, even though I wasn't fooled for a second. Then there was a very well-groomed computer programmer type, very promising. He noticed me right away, with that kind of provocative leer I find so irresistible. He entered the bathroom and I followed him, but the place was empty. Nobody by the urinals. The stalls had doors that looked straight out of a saloon in a John Wayne movie. Very badly lit. In the last stall I spied a pair of feet, in a very strange position, with the tips of his shoes facing the partition to the right. And this humble servant, of course, had her head pressed against the stall next door. The partitions, naturally, were pockmarked with holes. And like the snake in paradise with the red apple in his mouth, a hunk of male meat appeared through one of them. It still gives me the shivers whenever I think of it. I sucked him off until my eyelashes were bathed in come and paint bits that had chipped off the partition. Input, input, input. Sonofabitch. And then suddenly, someone pressed a switchblade against my jugular. Not a cry. Not a word. Threw me down onto the floor. I was beside myself. My mouth open, absolutely dumbfounded. The one with the knife was the scrawny, evangelical minister type. What fingers he had on him. He stripped me of everything in two seconds, the blade poised right over my heart. Such bastards, Mr. Policeman. For all the antiqueer laws you've got, tell me something: who are the real delinquents here? My God, I feel like Paul Newman in *The Verdict*. That little baby-face fooled me good: he nearly killed me with sweetness — not with some kind of trick, but with a flaming dickhead. And this humble servant walked right into the trap like an ass. What a nerve. I didn't dare scream, either. And then the computer guy and the evangelist just disappeared. They must have had a damn good celebratory fuck after that one. I, meanwhile, recounted my woes to the two spectacular black men and the chicano with the cherubic face, all of whom behaved like real sisters. First they treated me to a 7 Up to calm my nerves and then they took up a collection so that I could take a bus to my hotel. The chicano escorted me there, with no ulterior motives. In fact, the sweet young thing couldn't stop talking. Diarrhea of the mouth, as they say.

Now, what happened to me in Santa Barbara was exactly the opposite. This is it, Mr. Policeman. I'll finish off with this one. It's really remarkable what you can squeeze onto one of these cassettes if you speak fast enough. If you are concise. It fits. I mean, this story fits. Everything fits with me, everything. I'm referring, of course, to the tape recorder.

I realize that this last story is probably unnecessary. But it does make for a sensational finale. He was ideal. Silent. So, so silent. It all happened, as I was saying, in Santa Barbara. How I adore that city. How I adore that beach where everyone runs around playing volleyball. What bodies, girls, what bodies. What arms, what hands. I always end up absolutely cross-eyed after spending a day there. I do, of

course, have a favorite spot on the beach. Full of hot young
men. They cause quite a stir, I can assure you of that. That's
undoubtedly the reason I never get anywhere when I go
there. Too much noise as they pass the ball from one side of
the net to the other. What shrieking, what laughter. Then,
suddenly, oddly, I was totally immersed in a volleyball game
where nobody said a single thing. What heaven it was. Everything was so much more vivid. The net. The ball. The arms.
The hands. The torsos. The pecs. The asses. The massive
thighs. The feet. Those pendulous packages. I completely
lost track of time, and it got very late. The beach got emptier and emptier, and those men playing ball on and on,
oblivious to it all. As if they were somewhere outside this
world. Until suddenly one of them looked at his watch.
Eight o'clock. Horrors! The boy with the watch made a de-
finitive gesture. Let's go, he indicated. And all of them, oh-
so-disciplined. They didn't even glance at me. But this humble
servant followed their trail (how could she not?) until reaching a rather insipid bar. Too packed. There, to be honest,
they were nothing. There they were just part of the crowd.
The music was blasting. After a while, two of the boys from
the group — the cutest ones — motioned that they were leaving. They got up. They said good-bye. Those were my boys.
They left. I followed them. Suspense. Oh, how telegraphic
one can be, girls, nothing extraneous at all, nothing of the
sort. And before I knew it, the three of us were at a bar I
knew. A bar for queers, naturally. I almost cried from the
pure emotion of it all. *They will be mine,* I said to myself. Let
them see me. I had to get them to notice me. And they did,

of course, Colette is an expert at getting people to notice her.
The blonder of the two took a shine to me at first sight. He
smiled at me, and it wasn't as if we were sitting shoulder to
shoulder or anything. The place was packed. The blonder
one kept on smiling. And I smiled back, my mouth as wide
open as a garage door, and finally the other one got wind of
what was going on. They started gesturing with their hands.
What gestures. One of them closed his hand into a fist and
placed it inside his mouth, moving it up and down as if he
were playing a trumpet. He made himself clear. They were
dying for someone to suck them off. And naturally, I was a
willing volunteer. They kept on with the sign language, and
then started moving from the waist down, too. I nearly went
into cardiac arrest. Horrified. Just a little horrified, I mean.
They were overdoing it a bit, you know? I had to move closer,
to see if they would stop. I had to plow through that jungle
of sisters, and if my two suitors didn't stop moving like that,
everyone was going to know it. Rather embarrassing. It would
be dangerous, too—what if there were plainclothes policemen lurking about? Better for them to whisper it in my ear
and not make such a scene. One word was all it would take—
well, as it turned out, it didn't even take that. They didn't say
a single thing, girls. Not a peep. I got over to them, right next
to them, and they continued playing their trumpets. Just like
before. Without saying a word. Deaf and dumb. They were
deaf and dumb, girls, and they threw their big arms around
my shoulders as if I were their Morse code professor.

They were deaf and dumb, Mr. Policeman. The blonder
of the two lived in an adorable apartment in the Mission.

He slept on a water bed, very hedonistic, but we didn't even use the thing. We entered the house, went into the kitchen, and the two of them sat down at a pair of high bar stools. They sat with their backs to me and didn't even lower their sports briefs—they just took everything out through the leg holes, smiling all the while. And then one of them turned on the blender. I don't know what they were making—and in the state I was in, I didn't have time to figure it out. Bananas with honey, balls like California plums, bulky thighs like a cluster of wild grapes, knees as round as melons, ankles like baby pears, heels like ripe figs, butt cheeks as hard and sharp as a Texas accent—and then another serving of figs, baby pears, melon, another cluster of grapes, more California plums, and once again those bananas, this time bathed in Chantilly cream. And all of it in silence. Divine silence. Not a single word. For the entire time, the only thing you could hear was the sound of the blender, and when I finished them off and raised my head, the blender stopped and the blonder of the two offered me a brilliant smile and a giant glass filled to the rim with a fruit smoothie.

In silence. All three of us, very quiet, Mr. Policeman. Nobody made any comments; the encounter was free from the nuisance and betrayal of language. I swear to you, ladies, and I also swear to you, Mr. Policeman, that after enjoying such an abundant banquet, you could have cut off my tongue and I wouldn't have objected. Informational blackout, I think they call it.

# IV

*Where Finita Languedoc, also known as Miss Luxe, offers a melancholy, elegant tribute to maturity and the splendor of the golden years, and agrees to reveal her most prized secret in this celebration of the oral tradition*

I was a beautiful fourteen-year-old boy when Mama was widowed. Whenever you like, I'd be happy to show you photographs, and you can see for yourself that I was a teenager of golden curls and sea-blue eyes, very childlike and deliciously ambiguous, always dressed in truly exquisite taste by my stern nannies, who wore black uniforms with starched white aprons, patent-leather boots, and jaunty bonnets of the whitest piqué, always with a discreet bun pinned up underneath. Before Mama was widowed, she had one maid who worked exclusively for her — to wake her up in the morning, to draw her bath, to prepare her breakfast, her robes, her hairpieces, her frocks, her house slippers, her street shoes, her high heels for parties, her correspondence papers, her desk material, her schedule of daily events. And then there was a nanny for me. After Papa's death, however, they had to let the nanny go and Mama's maid had to look after me in addition to performing her other duties, a situation that was made worse by the serious lack of communication between the two of us.

"I am losing my patience," she declared to me one day, her nerves frayed by what she evidently perceived as the highly unpleasant task of preparing me for a walk along a tree-lined boulevard not far from where we lived. "It seems that nothing is ever good enough for you. You are far worse than your mother, which is saying quite a lot. And let me tell you something else: you might as well just dress like a little girl, so that everyone will know what to think of you for once and for all."

I assure you, her attitude was a bit uncalled for, but in those days maids with airs tended to indulge in the luxury of making a fuss over the least little thing. When it comes to respect and manners, we have simply gone to hell in a handbasket. I admit that I was a fastidious child, fascinated by all things beautiful, and extremely demanding with regard to my appearance. I had a particular weakness for high necklines and lace cuffs — I found them terribly becoming — and I was maniacal about my underclothes, always insisting on the most delicate and luxurious items, and absolutely intolerant of those ordinary undershirts and underpants that other people used, for I found them vulgar, bothersome, and indecent. And anyway, Mama's maid had to have grown accustomed to my attitude, for I'd inherited my refined sensibilities and firm character from Mama herself. And if I occasionally took things to a slightly irksome extreme, it was not because of bad character but because of aesthetics. My family motto was most clear with respect to this: in all aspects, servants were to possess an intimate understanding of perfection and were to treat their duties and obligations with the utmost love and devotion.

What with widowhood, of course, and our sudden financial dip, Mama suddenly found herself in a constant state of anxiety that teetered wildly and unpredictably between depression and compulsive activity. During her bouts of depression she would channel her emotions by slowly, languidly playing the accordion. It was an instrument for which she had shown a frightening aptitude from a very young age, despite the hundreds of piano masters who proved incapable of either burying the gusto inspired by such a proletarian instrument or channeling it toward something more respectable. In the more active phase of her anxiety, Mama would bemoan the state of the house, finding everything in hopeless disrepair but lacking the money to replace anything. I should mention, however, that our economic hardship was not a direct consequence of Papa's death but rather the result of a very unfortunate downturn in the business run by my grandfather—that is, my mother's father. In our house, which was the family estate, we had always lived on my grandfather's money, which came from his winery and the magnificent vintages it produced. But that year, sadly, everything went to pot, and when Papa died he left virtually nothing behind, mainly because he didn't do a thing while he was alive—he didn't even amass debts, he had, at least, been wise enough to send all our bills on to my grandfather.

Mama, however, was an only child who had been raised to appreciate the finer things in life, which inevitably cost a fortune. Thus her love for art and high culture, though admirable, was a somewhat expensive enterprise and cost the family dearly. As such, the poor thing had no other choice but to drown her sorrows in her accordion or else torture the maid, depending on her mood. The maid, in turn, tried to take out her own sorrows on me. A very unpleasant situation.

Mama's mourning attire could only be modest at best, although I should say that the maid knew her business and Mama did have a certain distinction and panache—after all, she was known for being one of the most refined, elegant ladies in the city. As such the results were not at all unpleasant, something that neither she nor I could have tolerated. As far as house visitors were concerned, she was rigorous in her selection of callers and placed a strict limit on their visits, which she received on Thursdays in the drawing room that overlooked the garden next to the carriages. After two months had passed she decided that the only person she'd allow to come and see her was her lifelong friend María del Carmen Marín, a single woman around Mama's age. María del Carmen Marín liked people to pronounce her last name with a French accent, in honor of her family's Gallic origins, an idiosyncrasy that constituted yet another bond between her and my mother, for my mother's maiden name is also of French origin and our family tree has roots in the Languedoc region. Moreover, María del Carmen Marín was an intellectual, educated woman who spoke several languages, wrote poetry, and occasionally published pieces in the opening pages of the *ABC* newspaper in Seville. On many afternoons, after tea time, she would read poetry as Mama played the *Sonate für Akkordeon* by Kaspar Roeseling or the *Danza di gnomi* by Fugazza, the only two pieces that in those days she felt able to play with the required level of virtuosity.

They dressed me in mourning attire as well, in a series of ghastly suits, though for five months I was scarcely allowed to leave the house. My French, violin, and fencing professors even stopped coming over, and only very rarely would I go for rides with my grandfather in his magnificent horse-drawn carriage that Mr. Julian, the driver, would steer through the newer areas of the Andalusian town of Jerez, through to La Rosaleda and El Bosque. My grandfather, the poor thing, was a very nervous type who was constantly scratching his groin area, which featured a large bulge that was always extremely hard. But since we always rode with the curtains down, nobody could see him.

Papa had died in January, and so summertime was deemed the appropriate moment to reassess our wardrobe and consider the possibility of lightening our—or at least my—mourning garb. In addition, it was an especially hot summer; the temperatures rose quite suddenly, much earlier than we had expected, and so all the windows and doors in the house were flung open throughout the day, so as to allow the air to circulate. That is, all the doors except the one that led to Mama's drawing room, on Thursday afternoons, when María del Carmen Marín came to call.

Now, I was horrified at the prospect of having to endure a plain, simple summer wardrobe, with no flair, no lace, no delicate edging, no velvet, bereft of all frills—which are, after all, the adjectives of a wardrobe, the things that give clothes their lyricism and style. Just thinking of it made me feel deathly ill, as though I had been stricken with blood poisoning. I had to fix this situation, because if I didn't I would surely die. There had to be a solution—lovely, original clothes for the summer wouldn't require that much material and so achieving my objective wouldn't require that much money, either. Just a little bit; I could easily take care of the rest with inspiration, plastic sensibility, and creativity.

I didn't have to look far: the maid was almost adorable in her summer uniform, a much lighter and more relaxed look than her serious, severe winter dress. With that winter outfit, in fact, the maid would never have done what I caught her doing surreptitiously one Thursday afternoon that summer. I caught her in a most compromising posture, her eye pressed against the lock of the door to the drawing room, where the sound of the accordion and the voice of María del Carmen Marín reciting poems had long since stopped. As we listened to some very strange, very feminine gasping noises emerge from the room, the maid moved her right hand back and forth under her petticoats at a velocity that made her look as though she had suddenly been struck with Parkinson's disease. When she caught sight of me she ran from the room, breathless, and as she scurried down the corridors she let out little yelps as if she were about to wet her panties and couldn't stand it any longer.

In winter, the maid looked like a Mother Superior in a uniform that radiated formality and seriousness. But in summer, at a quick glance, she looked like a woman who knew how to have a little fun in life. In her case, of course, I should note that the change of attire didn't cost a thing; Mama just recycled the previous year's uniform and the maid didn't dare complain. Although, who knows—perhaps that was why she started behaving so strangely, the way she did the day I caught her in the middle of her reverie. In my family we have always been hypersensitive to the details of our attire, an attitude that, I think, eventually became contagious among the servants. What I don't know, of course, is if the servants picked up other habits as well, and as isolated and trivial an incident as it may have been, I nevertheless found the maid's behavior vulgar and abusive.

In any event, I began to suspect that she had picked up on something special between Mama and María del Carmen Marín, because every Thursday afternoon the house would feel like a cauldron about to bubble over. Mama had ordered a pair of jet-black shirts to be cut and sewn by the older woman who had been coming to the house three times a week for ages, to take care of little unimportant sewing tasks. Oh, my heart still rankles inside me when I think of the humiliation Mama must have felt at not being able to hire a real seamstress. The resulting shirts, however, did give Mama a very unexpected look. It wasn't elegant, obviously—that was understandable; elegance would have been a minor miracle—but she certainly cut a glamorous, if somewhat common, figure. The proof was plain to see when Mr. Julian, the driver, was rendered absolutely dumbfounded upon laying eyes on her. It was a look that was a bit minimal, not at all sophisticated — quite tacky, actually — but it was so sensual and Mama needed it so badly that it became something of a catharsis for her. I don't know if it was the fluctuating temperatures, or Mama's anguish, or my grandfather's perpetual erection, or the virginity of Miss María del Carmen Marín, or the increasing shamelessness of the maid, or my own grief, but some of the most prized traditions in our house began to undergo a rather radical change that summer, and I have always felt that the detonating factors were two homemade shirts that Mama wore for the first time that summer.

I am aware that my previous comparison of a "cauldron ready to bubble over" is a bit typical and rather unworthy of a family that hails from Languedoc. I will amend, therefore, what I said before and will state, more appropriately I hope, that it was as if the air in that house had suddenly become infused with the hum of little bees, or the caws of doves in mating season. A decidedly exhausting atmosphere.

The days rolled by, one by one, with exasperating lethargy; the heat had a way of dissuading you from initiating any sort of physical or mental activity that might pass the time more quickly. Lunch became a painful, tedious ritual, and the food inevitably remained on the plates. My grandfather, as one might imagine, was nearly out of his mind. We would all retire for our siesta, and for just over half an hour the house would be suffused with a tranquillity that made it feel as if it were fermenting.

At around four o'clock, Mama would begin to play the *Sonate für Akkordeon* or the *Danza di gnomi* in her drawing room. Neither the heat nor the agitated atmosphere could stop her from playing that accordion. She spun her spider's web around everything with that perfect music; she was as haughty as a goddess of Osiris. To tell the truth, nobody ever complained about it out loud, but during those feverish summer afternoons, those melodies had a way of getting on one's nerves—mine, specifically. They lured me out of my room, and one day I wandered through the house still half-asleep, searching for a corner where I might find relief from the heat, a bit of fresh air. That was how I arrived at the small enclosed garden that led to the stables. To my shock, I discovered Mr. Julian there, completely nude and peering out from the main window of the stables—a low window whose bottom frame reached the middle of his thigh. With his gaze fixed on the balcony of Mama's drawing room, he anxiously followed her performance as he rocked back and forth in a frenetic sort of tribute, until his abundant white liquid spilled forth from the virile member that I was seeing for the very first time. It was worthy of a poetic ode.

As one might expect, I kept the discovery to myself, but from that afternoon on, I always tried to leave my bedroom and find a strategic hiding place in the garden before Mama's accordion began to play.

The scene was repeated every afternoon with almost frightening precision. The music would begin and Julian, as if catapulted from a spring, would appear at the window of the stables, stark naked — for a forty-year-old, he was such a handsome man — and he would instantly fall into a kind of trance, his eyes shining with the ecstasy of whatever he saw in that drawing room, and he would masturbate with true ferocity before my incredulous eyes, which were by now seduced forevermore by his vision. The melody playing that day will always be the most beautiful music I have ever heard, and the instrument the most perfect I have ever known. After Julian had emptied his barrels of masculinity he would quickly retreat from the window, and just as suddenly the sonata for accordion or the dance of the gnomes would lose its quiescence and splendor, though I am certain that only I experienced it that way.

Of course, the intrigue didn't end there. The first Thursday following my discovery, María del Carmen Marín added a few surprise elements to the spectacle of my mother and Julian enveloped in that accordion music. As one might imagine, I was terribly curious to see if Julian would dare to exhibit his magnificent attributes and masturbate in front of the window if Miss Marín was there. It was a pointless expectation on my part, because anyone less dense than I would have easily realized that the coachman was acting out in an unconscious state, in ecstasy, caught in an uncontrollable delirium. And anyway, Miss Marín seemed to me to be a real lady, aside from the minor eccentricities that are so typical in women of letters. And moreover, she wasn't forced to endure such unpleasant situations as that of mourning or economic hardship, nor did she find herself obliged to wear homespun shirts that could manage

to arouse the most irreproachable woman. There was no
reason at all that she would lose her composure in this type
of situation.

The accordion began to play. Julian emerged, naked,
and repeated his fascinating exercise, on cue. The tremulous verse of Rabindranath Tagore wafted from the lips of
María del Carmen Marín. All of a sudden I felt as though
my muscles were about to pop. And a rare bird, a bird that
seemed to be buried alive within the walls surrounding the
garden, began to chirp as if he had suddenly lost his mind.

This time, when Julian finished and disappeared from
sight, Mama's accordion and Miss Marín's voice suddenly
stopped cold. For an instant it seemed as if the entire world
had fallen silent. As if the universe had disintegrated altogether. I took a while to react, to realize that life went on,
that flames never burn in voids and are never extinguished
in a single moment, and to realize as well that *something*,
something very special, was most definitely taking place at
that moment.

Suddenly I recalled an image—a truly picturesque
vision of the maid in that peculiar position, spying through
the lock on my mother's drawing room door, shamelessly
abusing the feathery weight and restrained frivolity of her
summer uniform, burying her right hand in her petticoats,
as if searching for the fountain of wisdom. I began to run.
I bolted up the stairs three at a time until I reached the first
floor. And from the corridor, I saw her. There she was.
Just like the time before. Just like the previous Thursday.
Just like all the Thursdays that summer from then on.

Spying through the peephole in the middle of the lock. With that hand that wouldn't stop.

I tried to scream, but only the thinnest thread of a voice emerged from my mouth. "What are you doing there?"

It was enough to seriously frighten her. She ran out just like the time before, as if she was about to wet her pants. That was when I moved closer to the door, looked through the peephole, and saw everything.

Mama was sitting on the chaise longue, nude, her legs raised up high. María del Carmen Marín, dressed in that black shirt, was kneeling before her, burying her face like a madwoman in that special place where a woman becomes an oasis of gentle folds and dimples. The accordion, the venerable old scores by Roeseling and Fugazza, and the book by Tagore were all scattered across the floor. Mama laughed and cried boisterously, like a happy little girl, like a supermarket salesgirl after winning a million dollars in the lottery, like a Venezuelan bombshell as she is being crowned Miss World.

It was, undoubtedly, a revelation. A most intense experience. And even after all these years, I can still picture it so clearly. They never saw me spying on them, although I wonder if perhaps they sensed my presence on the other side of the door. I never told on the maid, either, and every Thursday I would let her watch for a little while, before I appeared in the corridor to ask in a tremulous voice, "What are you doing there?" just to scare her.

I, on the other hand, would watch them until Mama would have what looked like an epileptic attack before falling, almost unconscious, onto the chaise as María del Carmen Marín would withdraw her head a bit and rest it against the thighs of her lady friend. Then, wordlessly, I would retire to my bedroom and spend hours reliving the scene, back and forth, over and over. Many nights I would pretend to be indisposed at dinnertime and ask for a glass of milk to be brought up to my room. Mama never called the doctor and I doubt my grandfather ever realized that I hadn't turned up in the dining room.

During all those hours, my mind was gripped by apprehension. I was convinced that something was happening, something I didn't fully understand or realize the significance of. I knew that it was there, right before my very eyes, but I wasn't able to see it. I sensed that it might well be something of tremendous importance for me, for my future, for the rest of my life. And I cursed my inability to figure out what that "something" was.

The answer, as in so many life situations, came to me suddenly and for no apparent reason, after a brief flight of memory which zoomed in, for an instant, on a very specific moment in my mother's drawing room. I realized that María del Carmen Marín, as her lips had worked their way through my mother's laughter and tears, always wore that little black homespun shirt that created such a sexy, vaguely vulgar, look.

"Clothes," I told myself out loud, choked with emotion. "Of course. The answer is in the clothes."

And that was my second great revelation of the summer. That was how I discovered my vocation. "Languedoc. Haute couture."

Of course, discovering one's vocation is one thing—financing it is another. And this is where I shall once again reveal, for the very first time—specifically, I mean—my great secret.

It all began during one of those carriage rides that my grandfather and I would take through the outskirts of Jerez. As always, we rode with the curtains down while Julian, in the driver's seat, made sure to conduct the steeds at a graceful, relaxing clip. My grandfather spent the entire ride desperately tugging at his engorged member. Acute priapism, his doctor had declared. In the back of my head I have always thought I should build a monument, somewhere in the outskirts of Jerez, to that well-endowed son of Dionysus and Aphrodite, he of the merciless phallus.

"Grandfather, what's the matter?"

"I can't calm it down, my boy. Nothing works. The pain is killing me."

"Because of all the problems?"

"Yes, that's surely what it is."

That was when I decided it was time to make a full frontal investigation of my possibilities. I asked him:

"But aren't things improving, at least a little bit?"

"Well I suppose so, bit by bit."

That was when I decided it was time to lay my wager, and so I said,

"You know, I need to buy some clothes for summer."

He got very nervous at that. For a moment, I feared that I had ruined everything. But suddenly I realized that the look on his face was not one of fear but of trepidation.

Perhaps I could take the risk. I had nothing to lose, and so I decided it was now or never. My grandfather's breathing became unbearably labored and his eyes beseeched me more and more, surrendering to me. That was when I got down on my knees on the floor of the carriage — just as María del Carmen Marín had done in my mother's drawing room — and placed my hands on Grandfather's knees. Separating them just a bit, and I said to him,

"If I help calm you down a little, will you buy me some clothes?"

He didn't say a word. His hands trembling, he undid his trousers, tilted his head back, and closed his eyes as if awaiting decapitation.

He never said a thing. We would go out for a ride every afternoon and every so often Julian would discreetly park the carriage on the side of the road to La Parra. At the beginning, Julian never watched at all, but after a while he grew accustomed to the spectacle and one day Grandfather allowed him inside with us. Without any help at all, Julian somehow managed to position himself behind my back and locate the proper orifice through which to resolve his own erection, and in his moments of ecstasy he would hum the dance of the gnomes, which was easier for him than the German serenade.

I was lucky: my grandfather's business grew stronger, little by little. And that was how I acquired a beautiful closetful of clothes that summer and fully outfitted myself for the following winter, and for the winter after that as well. And then there was the Prince of Wales plaid suit I received when I turned eighteen, a short suit for the festival season and the Rocío holiday, and then a splendidly ruffled number for my more intimate celebrations, plus an evening outfit with rhinestone appliqués which I debuted on New Year's Eve the year I turned twenty. And then how could I forget the Carmen Miranda costume I wore for the carnival at Cádiz, and the outfit I took with me when I went to study in Italy, and then the entire wardrobe for my promotional tour of California, not to mention the complete spring-summer collection I presented four years ago at the inauguration of the Salon for Young Designers in Madrid.

Oh, how I miss him. I will never forget him. He taught me the treasures of maturity, the wealth of secrets that are the domain of the golden years. And this is why—despite the fact that no one believes me—I can truthfully say that I am simply dying to grow older, I'm dying to become an old man who can revel in the company of an abundant young man, as lovely as the adolescent boy I once was. And the young man who has the great fortune of knowing me will surely find happiness and all its rewards. And perhaps he, too, will live to tell about it one day, for some worthy cause just as I am telling my story now. Recently I have done just that for the very first time, and I'm sure Grandfather would understand.

Grandfather died in March of 1983. On his deathbed, he called for me. Just the two of us, alone. He banished everyone else from his room and asked me to lean over him, so that I could hear him speak. He was very thin, and the bedspread that covered him up to his lower belly no longer indicated the slightest swelling or hardness. That was when I understood all that I was about to lose, and it hurt me terribly.

Grandfather then whispered in my ear:

"Swear to me that you will never tell our story to Gutenberg."

Despite the cryptic nature of his request, I understood perfectly.

"I swear it," I said. "I may tell the story one day, for a good reason. But I will never put it on paper. That is strictly forbidden territory."

# V

*Where Miss Madelon, whose alias is an homage to another legendary dame with a predilection for the military profession, assures us that she eats and does anything and everything, though she will always have a special fondness for a particularly unique version of the joint Spanish-Portuguese maneuver*

Mr. Policeman, this one is for you. And I hope you like it, or are moved by it, at the very least. That is the purpose of all this, in the end.

The truth is, I have been in a bit of a quandary. It is not easy to select a story, as you may know, when you are a woman who has lived such an intense life as I have. I could tell you millions of stories, all of them fabulous, millions of flings, tremendous love affairs, all of them tumultuous and unforgettable. Just look at what happened to me yesterday. When I returned home there was a message to die for on my answering machine:

"Darling, I'm coming to Madrid this Sunday morning. Wait for me. I'm hot and ready for you, my love. I'm going to leave your ass like the rock of Gibraltar: your borders wide open and speaking fluent English."

As I listened to the message my lower body began to tremble and boil; I didn't know what to do with myself until that boy came and fulfilled his promise. Naturally, he had no need to identify himself. I recognized him right from the start, and that's no small feat—my answering machine is a bit old and distorts voices something awful, but I could never mistake the voice of Sindo Moreira Carballeira, swashbuckling gentleman paratrooper born in the town of Redondela, not even if it came to me tarred and feathered.

That message was what helped me decide which story to tell you. Oh, the things I could tell you about my Sindo. And I want to, so that the whole world will know, now while the news is still hot, that in a few short months Sindo will get discharged, and as soon as he becomes a civilian again he'll be gone with the wind, just like all the others. It's always the same story. Of course, replacements will begin to file in, and my inferior barracks do have a rather poor memory and welcome new recruits with open arms. But that doesn't mean I don't still go absolutely batty over every new man I meet and anyway, one always likes to think that *this* time around everything will be different.

Uniforms just drive me wild. I swear, I can't help myself. Just look at me right now, Mr. Police Chief of the State of Georgia: I'm picturing you in your regulation uniform—which I envision to be more or less like what cops wear in Hollywood movies. And believe me, I am getting horny already, I'm practically wetting myself. Doesn't that inspire you? Come on, don't play tight-ass with me, let yourself go, relax, get comfortable, turn off your desk lamp so that your office is shrouded in darkness, make sure your door is locked from the inside, and think of me for a moment. Think passionately of me, my darling. Picture me sitting next to you, kneeling down before you. I'm unbelievably thin, I swear it, I've got a perfect body that overflows only where necessary, in the places you like, in the places that all your boys like too. Take it from me, more than one of your big, studly blond boys already took me out back and you know it, you're jealous of it—didn't you overhear them talking about it amongst themselves? You know how these healthy young bucks get when they talk about certain things, I'm sure you can imagine how hot they get when they talk about me— they can't help themselves. Oh, and the way they laugh, the way they joke around and grab their overgrown, swollen cocks—the boldest ones of the bunch, in fact, simply pull their dick out of their pants because they can't take it anymore. Yes, that's right, right here in police headquarters, when they're on their breaks, when they're on night duty. You know it, you know perfectly well which of your young bucks have the most succulent cocks. And you know as well as I do that some of them can't even fit in my mouth, they're so big. Oh, you should be proud of your boys, Mr. Police Chief, they have such strength, one almost wonders if you didn't pick them out just for their hard bodies. And they say the most marvelous things about you, why, they love you to death. You're a very tight bunch, anyone could see that— the way you joke around with each other so naturally, it's easy to see those manly bonds between you and your boys. Of course, when they start talking about me they do go wild, they do tend to lose control of themselves. And maybe there are times when it embarrasses them a little, but they all seem to get over it quickly enough. And anyway, you know how they are, they can't help themselves. They see each other with their Jockey shorts gaping open, their huge, pulsating grenade launchers trembling in the open air, their hands nervous and fluttering, their eyes shining with anticipation, and then they reminisce about the pleasure I gave them, sometimes alone and sometimes in groups, while they were on patrol, you know. I mean, you know what goes on with your boys; they're so young, so strong, so seductive—it's perfectly natural. And I'm sure you can tell what a sensual, loving woman I am, and if you can't, I bet you wish you could. You have to try it out for yourself, darling; Miss Madelon is one unforgettable experience, just ask one of your boys. Just look at them, look at how they can't hold out anymore, that's why they're always gathering in little pairs, in little groups, to touch themselves, suck each other off. . . . They miss me, they need me, and they have to get by without me now but they still have to unleash all that energy somehow. It's natural, I tell you, they have to stick it somewhere hot, just look at them, look at how they drop their pants—it was with me they discovered the joys of the black kiss, the flavor of a swollen cockhead. Oh, how different and beautiful the world seems when they fuck you from behind, when they fuck each other without any inhibitions at all. You know it, you're no dummy—you want to try it too, of course you do, and that's why I'm here with you, sitting on top of your knees. Just look at me, can't you

see how wet I am? Look what you've done to me, Mr. Police Chief, it's monstrous, and it's all yours, really and truly
all yours. It's just as I imagined, and I knew you wouldn't
disappoint me, and a girl doesn't settle for just anything, you
know. A girl like me has intuition, a nose for things, and oh,
how good it smells. . . . Oh, let me do it, let me unzip you,
there, like that. . . . Ooh, how impressive. Now I see why
your boys are so happy with you, now I see why they adore
you so. What a joy to behold. . . . Time has left no mark on
this little gem—of course, I wouldn't want you to think I
was calling you old. I would never say that, for this is the
proof of a man's youth and you are young, so very young to
be the chief of police. And what balls, sir, what balls, just
the way I like them. . . . Oh, how I love it all. Let me bend
down a little, I want to see it up close, I want to kiss it little
by little as I get undressed. You don't have to do a thing,
don't even move, leave it all to me. Don't take anything off
at all, I don't want you to get undressed, let me do it the way
I like it . . . like that. I love this uniform of yours, I love its
stiff material, and if I stain it a bit, don't worry, it's just some
of my come, we'll get it out with some cold water; I release
a lot, you know, buckets of it, a real monsoon—that's how
I keep my cunt so smooth. You'll see what I mean when
you give it to me—don't get impatient on me, don't be a
little boy now. Your men are much more patient than you
are, you should ask them for a demonstration later on—
if you like it you'll learn fast. But right now, let me take
care of you, let me slide my tongue slowly over your inner
thighs. . . . Oh, how lovely, your hairs are standing up at

attention, how delicious. Mine are too, sir, I'm ready to melt away, you can't imagine how wide open my little hole is right now, you can't imagine how hard my little prick is. . . . All right, now you can do it, touch yourself a little bit, touch yourself while I rise up and position myself, yes, just like that. I want you to be comfortable, but don't take anything off, please don't unbutton your trousers, that's what drives me crazy—to embrace a man in a uniform while I'm completely naked. . . . Oh, it feels so good, and you're so strong, look what you've done to me. . . . Yes, now, carefully, cautiously, wait, I'm going to move now, let me sit on top of you. . . . Yes, yes, now I can feel it inside. All the way in, Mr. Police Chief, like that, uh-huh, tell me when, my darling, tighten it up, squeeze me, enjoy it, oh yes, enjoy it the way I do, and go ahead, whisper some sweet nothings to me. . . .


There you have it. I'm calmer now. And I hope you've calmed down a bit too. I'm crazy about orgasm. After an orgasm you can send the Inquisition after me, and the whole Georgia police force. It wouldn't faze me a bit.

Now that I've refreshed my Silicone Valley, I feel like new. Ever since I read in the papers that there's a place near San Francisco they call "Silicone Valley," I've been thinking that I should petition them to take me on as their adopted daughter. I always imagined it was a place filled with transvestites, because of the name, but apparently it is a land filled with computers. How awful. It doesn't matter, though—it is still a marvelous name as far as I am concerned; to me it still sounds like the paradise of the queers and you know me, I'll stop at nothing to get them to adopt me. Of course, Colette la Coco, who is a virtual pro in your tongue, Mr. Policeman—don't get all hot under the collar, I'm referring to your language, English—tells me that I've got it all wrong, that it's actually called Silicon Valley, not Silicone. How preposterous. [Voice of la Coco: "Ass."]

All right, it's time to move on, I suppose. I will act as though I did not hear that last interruption. You do the same, Mr. Police Chief. Let us not be bothered.

I was explaining how those uniforms turn me into a shameless hussy. And the stiffer the better—or the worse, depending. I suppose my age and my stringent diet have a way of weakening my defenses and I have to compensate somehow. As far as my age—well, I'd rather not think about it, but my diet, of course, is surely going to be the death of me. How awful. I despise it. I despise going through life depriving myself of things. Freedom is one of the things I prize the most, I am a staunch defender of freedom, nobody can take that away from me. The problem is, freedom is so horribly fattening. . . . I mean nutritional freedom, of course, don't get alarmed. The other freedoms, the real kinds, the truly beautiful kinds, are divinely becoming. I'm not saying that one shouldn't control oneself at times, Mr. Police Chief, but one should be able to control oneself freely, at one's will, and not because someone has placed a gun to one's head. Not you or anybody else.

There is one more thing I wanted to clarify with respect to uniforms and diets. I don't want you to think that I am inflexible. My God, no. On the contrary. As far as leisure time—the pleasures of the flesh, I mean—I don't give it a second thought. This girl eats everything. It's just that uniforms are my favorite dish.

To give you an idea, as soon as the Madrid jai-alai season begins, I prepare my answering machine with plenty of backup tape. Every Monday, without fail, my poor baby receives the same call and subsequently saves the following message:

"Hey, it's me. Can I come over?"

Not one syllable more, ever. Not for Christmas, not for the New Year, not for Groundhog Day. And you should hear his tone of voice. Always the same seven words, as if he had to put on special dentures to say them, as if no one ever taught him any words other than those. This one doesn't have to identify himself, either. He's the forward. A really nice person, actually, and always very grateful when it's over. The least little thing gets him out of his pants, the poor thing. His name is Jesús María, though his teammates call him little Baby Jesus, and apparently he is a regular prodigy. I mean he's a real ace with the ball, he's got a reputation for being quite a champion in his field. Sometimes he comes to my house with his bottle man—the man in charge of supplies, that is, something I clarify for you here because I don't want you getting any strange ideas and because it's always worthwhile to expand one's vocabulary—and I enjoy those encounters even more, what do I have to hide? The bottle boy's name is Iñaki, like all of them, although this one is from some small town called Fermoselle, in the province of Zamora.

He's short and stocky, but he has a bod made for sinning and a jar of linament between his legs that takes my breath away—I don't even notice the other one, and this humble servant girl always ends up singing his glories when it's all over. Actually, it has been quite some time since they last came to see me—perhaps they've moved to another country. The last time I saw little Baby Jesus he was very distracted because he had received an offer to play jai-alai in Tijuana, and the poor baby didn't know what to do. If they did, in fact, leave, they must be missing me, because everyone tells me that the ladies in Mexico are a very traditional bunch.

Of my soccer players, the one who left me with the fondest memories was a boy from La Palma, in the Canary Islands, who came to Madrid after getting selected by the Rayo soccer team. He went back to his island after the season ended—the only playing time he ever got was when he was called in to substitute for another player for twelve minutes during the King's Cup. To keep in shape, the poor darling would come and visit me. He was delicious, and the way he worked me over . . . he could've marketed and sold himself like hotcakes in a department store. But he suffered from depression, as one might expect, and at the end of the day all he ever wanted to do was cuddle up next to me and kiss the inside of my hand as I stroked his back.

In any event, he was most certainly a professional, despite his run of bad luck here. And let me tell you, Mr. Police Chief, let God—or at least the police of the State of Georgia—save us all from amateurs. I've learned my lesson. From one nervy sonofabitch in particular. That one ended

up in the gutter, but he couldn't help it. It's not something
I'm particularly happy about—I do still have a heart, you
know. But sometimes life gives you exactly what you deserve. Not always, and not with everyone, but this man got
exactly what he deserved. He was a boy with a lot of body
and a lot of presence, very full of himself, a good-looking
blondie, a real charmer, if you know the type. A boy spoiled
by his single mother, hopelessly conceited, so flattering it
was almost sickening. He couldn't say a single honest, sincere word—it was as if he didn't want to set a precedent or
something. My God, he could have fooled the morning sun,
that little thing. A real little pig if there ever was one. And
this humble servant girl, despite it all, was whipped. You
know how things can get. When I met him he told me he
was a soccer player. The only soccer that idiot ever played
was a couple of weekend games with his friends in the neighborhood, but that was enough to make him think he was the
next Pelé. He was a horrible fuck, but then, sometimes one
loses one's senses. And I was desperately proud of this boyfriend who drew so much attention to himself. I introduced
him to all my girlfriends, and one of them, who has a fasci-
nation with history—we call her Miss Preterit or sometimes
just Miss Backwards—was very impressed with him. She
went so far as to declare that he looked like an officer in the
Prussian army, even though I think they ceased to exist eons
ago. Who cares, anyway, God only knows what stone that
little angel crawled out from. To make a long story short,
one day I discovered him cheating on me with a butt-ugly
queer who worked as a makeup artist in a beauty parlor.

And so we broke up. The pig didn't even get upset, or at least not in my presence. He ended up finding a job as a salesman, selling milk to supermarkets—pasteurized milk, nonfat milk, skim milk, milk of every shape and color you could imagine. After a few months he was transferred to Málaga, and that was the end of him. There, he met a German man, married, who owned a milk-shake company, and he started seeing him—that is, in between dates with the rest of the queer population of the Costa del Sol. One day, while they were sixty-nining each other, the German's wife appeared and fired a giant pistol straight into her husband's head. The milkman was affected in his nether regions, and I don't think the doctors have been able to do much more than mutilate him even further. It all came out in the tabloids, front page and everything, with the most ghastly photos.

Such a sad story, isn't it, Mr. Police Chief?

I despise sad stories, actually—I don't know what came over me. I suppose it's one of those things that you lock up inside you even though it inevitably comes rushing out when you least expect it. I don't know if he still works in the same line of business, but after that scandal, I can only imagine that his girlfriend at the time, the poor thing—they were about to get married!—probably sent him packing. I pray to God that she doesn't suffer half the bitterness and loneliness that he does.

Smiles, Mr. Policeman, smiles, for goodness' sake. How did I get myself all caught up in that? I didn't even mean to tell you about that. . . . What I wanted to talk about was my Sindo. He's a good one, you'll see. How grand to have received such a gift in the great lottery of life, to help heal my wounds.

The first time I invited him over, we were in the taxi and he said something to me, utterly unconcerned that the driver might be able to overhear us.

"I'm going to spread your ass as wide as a birdbath, baby."

I loved it. He was full force already; when I glanced down I could see the buttons on his pants straining, threatening to burst open. I also liked how he went straight to the point, very direct, nothing at all like the milkman and his boring little cat-and-mouse game. And did he hit me up for money afterward? Well, yes, naturally. This humble servant girl has nothing at all against giving money to a lovely little thing after he's worked her body over so very well. Now my friends here are making these very shocked faces, as if I've scandalized them. *We never pay for it,* they say. Whatever. Maybe they don't pay in cash — oh sure, they fool themselves into thinking that they don't need to scrounge for loose change when they need a good fuck, but just take a look at their restaurant, gas station, and clothing store receipts and you'll get a pretty good idea of how much they spend on men every month. And that's not even mentioning the real expenses — apartments, cars, motorcycles. And Mr. Policeman, the money one shells out on these men is not tax-deductible — I don't know why, of course, it's outrageous when you consider that these are necessary ex-

penses for maintaining one's sexual equilibrium, which after
all is a health issue—and anyway, at the end of the day, who
is going to go around collecting receipts, with tax included,
for this sort of thing? I say it is far better to pay for these
studs in cold hard cash, fifteen or twenty bucks a fuck, and
stop driving yourself nuts over it. I should know—take that
milkman, for example. He didn't charge me a cent for his
services but I paid dearly for his love. That sonofabitch
practically depleted my savings account, which is all I've got
to take care of me in my old age.

"When I'm through with you your ass is going to be
like the gorge at Ronda," he whispered in my ear as we rode
up in the elevator, shoving his hand clear through my last
line of defense—that is, my panties. "Anyone who sees you
from behind is going to get vertigo."

Vertigo was what I was getting right about then. Clearly,
the kid had a way with words. And he clearly had a way with
everything else; that was evident. That little angel's bodywork was not to be imagined, Mr. Policeman—I noted this
as I started getting ready for our final number.

Some people make the biggest fuss over the topic of
prostitution. I don't understand it; as much as I try, I simply don't understand it. My God, everyone's trying to sell
you something in this life, Mr. Policeman: those who have
talent sell talent, those who have college degrees sell knowledge, those who celebrate mass sell salvation. Everyone does
it. And those who have only their bodies to sell, well, that's
what they sell. And why should we think them worse than
the rest of us, if the thing they sell—their bodies—is sup-

posedly so much baser than what other people sell? Because if we're all selling, aren't those people who sell things like talent, art, culture, medicine, or religion really much worse than the people who sell a simple piece of meat? It's so obvious and clear to me, I just don't understand what the witch-hunt is all about.

"Your ass is going to look like Khadafy's turban when I'm through with you," said my Sindo, nudging me from behind with his meaty prod as I desperately tried to open the door, which I couldn't seem to do on account of my nerves. "I'm going to leave you looking like a real Arab turban. Big enough to fit Mohammed inside, kicking and screaming, baby."

Gasping and panting was more like it, Mr. Policeman, you can't imagine the pleasure. What a way my Sindo has in bed. I still remember all the details, of course. He was so eager to indulge, he practically ate me alive, I swear it. You can't imagine how wild he went over my breasts. And he still does, every time he comes over. His mouth is just like a feather pillow, so soft. He bites gently at my nipples and whispers sweet nothings in my ear in gallego, bathing my body in a warm glow — so delicate, so delectable. Gallego is such a sweet-sounding language, Mr. Policeman, and making love to the sound of it is divine madness. You don't have to understand a word of it. I don't — I never understand a thing Sindo says when he drowns me in kisses from head to toe. Oh, how he loves it. He doesn't let me move an inch, you see, and in this first stage he doesn't even take his clothes off. Sometimes I have to close my eyes so as not

MISS MADELON                    131

to get dizzy, and then after a while I can't resist him any
longer, that adorable sweetheart in his uniform (sometimes
complete with hat), and I just want to swallow him down
whole, no biting or chewing, just one big gulp. Madness.
I have to close my eyes. It's always been like that, ever since
the first day. Since the very first time he came to my house
and took me in his arms like a virgin bride and asked me,
"Where's the bedroom? Where is there a mattress in
here?" No beer, no chitchat, no "Can I use the bathroom?"—
no pretensions at all. Simple and straightforward, and he
tore off the cute little number I had put on—ripped it to
shreds, in fact, but I could have cared less. I was thrilled—
what luck to have come across a sadist, I told myself, this
was precisely what I needed to forget about the last man,
the milkman. Because love, no matter how misguided, is not
so easy to recover from. And though my Sindo has not fully
erased my memory of the milkman, I don't know if anyone
could. Only time, a little tenderness, and tranquillity will
help my wounds to heal, Mr. Policeman. My Sindo was
simply the impetus that pushed me out of my inertia. The
poor thing was so worked up when we got into the taxi that
by the time we made it to the bedroom—so white, so clean,
so ideal—he simply exploded. A question of youth, of course,
but he perked right back up, just like a resilient baby lamb.
Oh, the affection that poured from the lips and the finger-
tips of that boy, that swashbuckling gentleman paratrooper,
that angel who came down from heaven to savor every last
bit of me—except for my fearsome Bermuda Triangle, of
course. That is sacred territory; for many years now, I have

availed myself of a very exclusive line of panties that leave the entire battlefield open from behind and fully concealed from the front, so that my secrets remain well-kept and off-limits to even the most persistent suitors, who inevitably try to persuade me to show it to them, to take it out because they want to see it, they want to suck it off, et cetera. Degenerates. Not worth discussing. One has to maintain certain principles, after all. And since I feel that I am a woman, psychologically speaking, I feel that my protuberance goes against my personal psychology. Getting rid of it for good, of course, is a rather frightening prospect, so I'd never do that, but I certainly don't take it out and show it to people. I simply act as though it doesn't exist. My Sindo knows. I mean, he knows that it doesn't exist, he understands. He understood right from the very first day, devouring me everywhere but there—front and back, up and down—and when he turned me around and leaned down toward the fortress where I guard my munitions, when he arrived at the battlefield, he stopped and stared, as if he had just encountered one of the wonders of the world. And then, in a tone of voice that revealed the awe and emotion he felt, he said, in gallego, the language of his people:

"*Carallo, esto bota fumo.*" In other words: "Damn, that thing is smoking."

Ever since that day, my Sindo refers to my fortress as the *botafumeiro* and my battlefield as the cathedral of Santiago de Compostela. And sometimes, he leaves a special message on my answering machine to that effect:

"I'm going to leave your ass like the cathedral of Santiago with the *botafumeiro* smoking away inside, on the day of the Holy Apostle."

And he always keeps his word. Oh, how he keeps his word. The way he fills me up, why, you couldn't get a shred of incense inside me. I get dizzy from the way he rocks me, so hard, so good.

When the wave of spasms finally subsides, he asks me: "Are you all right, my little whore?"

"A bit queasy, actually."

"Well, that's nothing compared to the butterflies you're going to get with the guy who replaces me. I told you before, I'm going to leave your ass like the gorge at Ronda."

"That's all right," I say, preparing myself, "I'll buy a lifetime supply of Dramamine if I have to."

The truth is, Mr. Policeman, I know I'll eventually have to find a substitute for my Sindo. Not because I'm so incredibly perverted, but because those are the facts of life. My Sindo will get discharged from the military and he'll eventually want to ship out. That's the way those boys from Galicia are, I'm afraid. They've got a girl in every port and at any given moment they just up and leave, and head out to all corners of the earth. I have no future with him. I know it. I'll put his photo in my album, a photo of him in his paratrooper's uniform, and when I'm an old lady I can entertain myself thinking of him. Thinking of him and of all the others.

I think a successor is already in the works. He hasn't said it in so many words, but I can tell. And if you think

about it, that's nothing to sniff at. It's a very practical touch.
He'll leave me in good hands, and at the same time he'll be
doing a favor for a friend, someone he trusts. The friend,
specifically, is a redhead from Totana, in Murcia, a boy
whose heart beats with all the brio of the open fields and
whose cock is worth more than a year's harvest.

He broke it to me suddenly, about a month ago. As
always, the news was delivered via answering machine.

"Darling, we're going to leave your ass like the Rock
of Gibraltar." Et cetera.

I rewound to make sure I hadn't misheard the message.
But no, it was clear as a bell. My Sindo, as naturally as ever,
had said "we."

Well, why should I deny it, Mr. Policeman—it excited
me. A bit of variety always helps, always titillates, always
does a world of good. As I washed my angina a bit—that is
how my friend Pamela Poodle, who is here with us today,
refers to it. Harebrained Pamela Poodle, always mixing up
her terms, insists that her doctor tells her that she has a bit
of an angina down there, a baby angina, but a real one nevertheless, just beneath her balls. Right, just like the Aunt
Angina pancakes she makes for Miss Marcuse in the morning. Anyway, as I tried to imagine what the second boy was
like, I started getting horny right there on the bidet, and I
practically came all over the tile floor.

Luckily, I controlled myself. My intuition told me not
to waste any of my precious energy. My intuition is like a
little bell on the front door of my brain: it always warns me

in time. There is nothing like good intuition. Because that day, reality surpassed all possible expectations.

The "we" wasn't two. It was four.

Sindo arrived with three men: a Spaniard—the redhead from Totana—and two unbelievable Portuguese men. The boy from Totana was named Fermín and had a face like one of Salzillo's angels. Of the two Portuguese men, Vitor Manuel had blond hair and green eyes and came from Oporto, while the other one, who called himself Alex, was a scandalously dark and handsome type from Faro, though I could swear he must have had some African blood mixed in at some point. The two of them were doing their military service in Coimbra, and they had just finished performing a round of joint Spanish-Portuguese maneuvers. And there they were, in my house, perfectly happy to be there, because as Sindo said when he introduced them, they had become friendly during the war.

My Sindo always says hello with a deep French kiss, no matter who he's with. The one from Faro—who I quickly realized was a clever little kid—didn't want to left out of the running from the get-go, as they say in those TV sports shows, and stuffed his tongue into my mouth, practically down to my tonsils. The one from Totana was a little shy and his face was beet-red as he kissed me on the cheeks like a modern-day cavalier. The little angel from Oporto kissed me like an old-fashioned gentleman would, on the hand. And I, to keep the game going, threw myself on top of him and kissed him next to his ear. And then he, without missing a beat or losing the least bit of his formality, tossed his head back jauntily and said,

"*Obrigado.*"

Whiskies all around, naturally, whiskies for everyone. I always keep a stocked bar. And I also happen to have a perfectly charming apartment. Things being what they are, of course, it isn't half as gorgeous as that of Colette la Coco, but she is a top executive, after all. And it may not be in as luxurious a neighborhood, either, but it is cozy, very clean, and only steps from the center of town. The soldiers, poor things, they love it. Compared with a military barracks, it's Buckingham Palace. They feel instantly comfortable, instantly at home in my place. They look around and touch everything that strikes their fancy. I show them my photos, my press clippings, my work clothes. It always makes quite an impression. Occasionally I'll invite them to the club to watch my show, and they always cause quite a stir among the cast, a wild bunch of drag queens. Normally I don't invite my boyfriends to see my show unless I've got them on a tight rein and can make sure that they won't get carried away. But I took the Portuguese men with me the very first night, girls, for I didn't want to waste such a golden opportunity, the market being what it is. The poor babes were veritably drooling when they got a load of how elegant and luxurious the club was, not to mention the various attractions. And with me as the star of the show, no less. A top figure in my field, Mr. Policeman, if I might say so myself.

You have to see me out there for yourself, Mr. Policeman. Out there and in private quarters as well. Just ask the
Portuguese fellows, if they ever turn up in your part of the
world, executing those joint maneuvers of theirs. Just ask
them and you'll run out to buy a ticket to Madrid. And I'll
be here waiting for you.

Of course, perhaps you'd prefer to execute some maneuvers with the Portuguese men. You and them alone, I
mean. You won't regret it, I can assure you of that. Allow
me to elaborate.

As soon as he downed his first whisky, my Sindo declared that the bed was going to be far too small for us, and
suggested that we clear out the living room and get comfortable on the floor, with the sofa cushions. He showed me
what he meant. First he turned the rug upside down, as if
searching for enemy planes, and then he unbuttoned his
pants faster than a speeding bullet, but without taking anything off. Alex, the one from Faro, followed suit — clearly
this kid had sworn to his superiors that he wasn't going to
let himself be intimidated by any Spaniard. He even tried
to muscle his way into the role of squadron leader: whereas
my Sindo wore a perfectly awful pair of khaki Jockey shorts
under his trousers (courtesy of the armed forces), that im-
pulsive Portuguese fellow wore nothing at all. And I know
he did it on purpose: as soon as he unzipped himself, a massive mortar fell out, as dark and hard as the Cold War, and
he gaily began to play with himself. As a skirmish maneuver I found it a bit risky, but this world is not for the weak,

after all. The boy from Totana, meanwhile, had sat down in lotus position — I don't know if that's a regulation military move, but it was so tender. He unbuttoned himself, yes, but without the easy release of the Portuguese move, given the protective positioning of his legs. Of course, I should note that the bulge in his pants did reveal quite a package, which he could hardly hide forever, as I learned later on. The one from Oporto was the last to take his place in the formation. Before he did so, he asked me in a very genteel manner if I would mind sitting in the center of the rug. I did so without a second thought and loosened up my lingerie, to make sure my body was nice and comfortable for what lay ahead. And then something utterly unexpected happened: in about a split second he was buck naked.

"Jesus Christ!" I exclaimed. That had been a full-blown attack, with heavy artillery.

Naturally, I surrendered. I succumbed to them easily, with the joie de vivre of an Italian battalion. In a heartbeat my panties were up around my Adam's apple, my legs raised up high. That was when that little firestarter Vitor Manuel dropped his gentleman act right away — there he was, the chief of staff, attacking me with the most violent thrusts imaginable. What thrusts they were. What speed. In less than three minutes I felt my insides ripped through like Vietnam after the Americans landed. And then the one from Oporto withdrew, ever so gently, filled with emotion, and as they all reassumed their original positions, he became a gentleman again.

"*Obrigado,*" he said.

Very *obrigado,* I thought. That was the last real thought
I had, of course. After that, there was no time to think at
all. Oh, it was war, Mr. Policeman—those joint Spanish-
Portuguese maneuvers are something else. Before I knew
it, the kid from Faro was in my mouth, down my throat, all
the way down my trachea. What throat action it was. What
an assault, what total penetration. The one from Faro was
on top of me, spilling every last drop of milk he had, and he
didn't take it out, or say thank you, or anything. What persis-
tence. What ambition. What ferocity. And I was in heaven,
of course. I did ask Sindo for some backup, but luckily it
was unnecessary. In these parts, Mr. Policeman, joint maneuvers are quite serious. And my Sindo is a responsible
soldier. He knew what his duties were, and fulfilled them
brilliantly. With the bravery and valor for which he is known,
he relieved Vitor Manuel of Oporto in my rearguard trenches.
What joy. I must send an urgent communiqué to military
headquarters—those boys deserve a decoration. All of them.
All four. I wouldn't want you to think that the boy from
Totana tried to slip away, even though at first he seemed as
timid as a mouse. Not on your life. He reared up like a wild
boar before too long. He told the one from Faro that his time
was up—he had come twice already, like a randy orangutan
at that, and it was his turn now. He, Fermín of Murcia, son
of Petra . . . Oh, how proud his mother would have been. He
had to prove his valor, risk his life, conquer the enemy camp,
achieve great honor, earn the cross of San Hermenegildo, and
proudly pin it on his army jacket. He was prepared to maintain his post at the upper guard for as long as it was neces-

sary. But they didn't let him, not even for five minutes. The
one from Faro wanted the lower guard so badly he would've
killed for it. Ah, what a beautiful spectacle, two warriors
engaged in hand-to-hand combat for the same cause. And
that cause, of course, was my Rock of Gibraltar, my Ronda
gorge, my Khadafy turban, my beloved birdbath. On the
other hand, the source of the conflict was my own weapon,
my Pandora's box, my throat. The one from Oporto juiced
it up for the third time, and as he withdrew, panting, he
sputtered,

"*Obrigado.*"

All told, almost sixteen successful skirmishes between
the four of us.

Take it from me, Mr. Policeman; if these Portuguese
paratroopers ever show up in your neck of the woods to
execute a few maneuvers, don't let them get away. Be
tough on them. Lock them up in your headquarters as fast
as you can, don't tell a soul, and take full advantage of the
opportunity.

Of course, my Sindo might get to you first. Don't give
me that look, now. There's nothing so odd about this. My
Sindo, as you know, will be getting his license in a few
months, and he'll be wanting to take off shortly afterward.
He's from Galicia, and God only knows how far afield he'll
go. He might just make it to Georgia, although it's a long
trip across that ocean. But those men from Galicia are a re-
sourceful bunch, so don't be surprised if Sindo calls you
someday. I can tell you already what he'll say to you. Maybe
he'll even leave a message on your answering machine — he

loves to do that. So listen closely. And don't forget it, because you won't want to let him go. You'll recognize it right
away anyhow, because no one else in the world can say it
like he does. He's the best. So listen up, because when my
Sindo calls you, Mr. Policeman, he'll say,

"Sweetheart, I'm going to leave your ass like the Rock
of Gibraltar, your borders wide open."

You won't be disappointed.

# VI

*Where Pamela Poodle, also known as Miss Walking Disaster for her disastrous tendency to call things as she sees them, offers a paean to sincerity and confesses the true nature of her dream life*

Oh, Mr. Policeman, I really didn't want to get involved with this. Really, truly, there's just no point to it. I have nothing to tell you, honestly, nothing. I'm trouble, I'm what they call irrepressible and unconscionable, because I have utterly no qualms about speaking the truth about things.

Of course, my lady friends scoffed at me, saying, "Sure, go ahead and do that if you think it will save you." They say that your laws don't make distinctions and that all you people need is a whisper of suspicion to nab someone—and I admit, I'll certainly give you a whisper of suspicion, but my God, a girl can't simply change her appearance and behavior overnight, like the man in *The Metalpsychosis*, or whatever that novel is called, the one where the guy turns into an insect, you know which one I mean. The tiniest hint or insinuation is all they need to interrogate you down to the hemline of your panties? What injustice, my God. You have to understand the kind of queer that I am. You have to understand the truth about me, because I haven't exercised my inclinations at all, I haven't done anything, anything at all. Let me explain why.

In the first place, because I'm going through a terrible dry spell, I mean months and months of total abstinence — well, *almost* total, to be completely truthful. If it weren't for my dogs I wouldn't have money to buy a cup of coffee. My dogs are the one thing that save me when things get the way they are now. They are two adorable little poodles, Mr. Policeman, a boy and a girl. The girl is called Poli, after Pola Negri: she has that face — you know, that innocent but devastating look — and though she's tiny, almost a miniature, she has been absolutely prophetic. What I mean is, she gets pregnant at the drop of a hat, thank God. The boy poodle is called Fairie, diminutive for Fairbanks — like Douglas, Mr. Policeman, and please forgive the pronunciation. It's not that he's a degenerate poodle, mind you, he just has very active hormones, and so the minute Poli gives him the least little hint he humps the hell out of her. You men don't have anything against that, do you? Because my poodles obey the rules governing matrimony laid down by the Holy Roman Church — no unsanctioned positions or anything. They just get a bit carried away with the impulses given to them by Mother Nature, who is wise but wild in her own way. Contraceptives, of course, are out of the question — most especially in the case of young couples, of course, and my little dogs are mere babies. Though, that said, I *have* been told that poodles are a rather precocious breed, and little Poli has already been through quite a bit for her young age—she's given birth on five separate occasions now, and each puppy is worth a good five hundred dollars. So you can see, it's not enough to make me a millionaire or anything—I'm actually thinking that I'm going to have to replace her with a puppy from her litter, something that makes me feel both sad and, well, odd, because when it comes to ethics I have always been quite scrupulous.

So the point is, anyone can understand that I don't have the kind of income that would allow me to spend my days and nights flirting and batting my eyes at the men on the Gran Vía. Because my bad-mouthing friends here like to call me—rather mercilessly, I might add—the Dog Doctor. But what else am I to do? They're my only way out, and I'm not about to go and ingest a vial of sleeping pills like Marilyn.

Some people tell me that if that's how I see things, I should get my head examined. But it's very easy to talk and talk when you have a good job and a good salary and a more or less guaranteed retirement fund. At other moments in my life, naturally, I had marvelous jobs—I started out working as a majordomo in a very high society house in Palma de Mallorca, but I wanted more for myself, and so I came to Madrid to try my luck in the movies, to fulfill my lifelong dream. I have been reading *Fotogramas* magazine for over thirty-five years now, even though it's gotten outrageously expensive and the quality has gone down the toilet, and all they ever write about is videos and more videos. . . . Videos, to my mind, are something extra, something, as the Gospel says, that shall be added unto you. In any event, my attempt at fame was a dismal failure, and I spent my life savings opening up a dry cleaning outfit that didn't even last two months, and ever since then I've gone from one job to another until I finally ended up involved in this business with the dogs, for lack of anything better. Perhaps I have too many fantasies and too few brain cells, but everyone has the right to take a risk: success and failure are also a question of luck.

Many aspects of my life have suffered in this *Vía Crucis* I have endured for the past fifteen years, most notably my hair and my digestion, and those are the other two reasons why I live my life, in sexual terms at least, like a Trappist monk. As far as my hair is concerned, I've tried everything — lotions, massages, shampoos, daring haircuts, bizarre concoctions and herbal infusion treatments, everything. Useless, all of it. And once I couldn't hide my balding any longer, I tried toupees and wigs, but unfortunately I could only buy the inexpensive kind, because that was when I was going through my roughest period, financially speaking, and that remedy turned out to be worse than the illness. Nowadays they say that certain transplanting and hair-weaving techniques can work miracles, but they cost a fortune, and I don't know what good it would do me to have a gorgeous mane of hair and not be able to go anywhere or do anything. And so I get by with my various and sundry headpieces: cloches, berets, ski caps, Borsalinos, Panama hats, depending on the mood and the occasion. I take very special care of this little detail, although I do have to take them off when it's time to eat, a rather dicey venture. Well, I used to take extra-special care of this issue, because by now all my hats are hopelessly out of style, although I do try to convince myself that anything goes nowadays when it comes to fashion. And I ask you, Mr. Policeman, how can I drop my trousers for a man without decanting, if you know what I mean? And if I don't decant? That is, if I don't remove my chosen hat? Excuse me, occasionally I take to using words straight out of the dictionary—the only luxury I can allow myself these days is the luxury of culture and the intellect. How, then, can I find the necessary freedom of movement required by fraternity with my fellow man, to put it delicately? I have always felt that during an oratory event, revealing a head as bald as an airport runway could shock and kill even the most resilient microphone, if you know what I mean. And do note that I try to speak in metaphors so as not to offend you.

My other problem, digestion, could have truly dire consequences with respect to this. Everyone tells me that constipation is never a good thing, but it has become a chronic issue and I have never been able to solve it. Always, ever since I was a little girl, I have been a victim of severe abdominal cramps. One queer doctor, with whom I had a brief romance, blamed it on my family's eating habits. But then, when I really began to hit some rough times, idiot that I am, I encouraged my anal-retentiveness, thinking that it would help me take fuller advantage of the food I ate. And now I suffer the consequences. In addition to cold sweats and general aches, which flare up on an hourly basis—why, it feels as though my little poodles are squabbling away inside of me—I live with the feeling that my pipes are packed to the gills, like an overstuffed public bus, like a subway car at rush hour, and you can't exactly sell tickets if your vehicle is overbooked. Not to mention the fact that I'd be exposing myself to certain violence as the result of the ensuing flatulence. They'd call me a pig, or worse.

No, sir. I would die of embarrassment.

And so, Mr. Policeman, you now know my truth. I used to think that being honest was never worth the trouble, but around here we know that you do what you have to do. From what I can tell, however, this fuss you've made, ranting on about health issues and proper behavior, is nothing less than a witch-hunt, exactly like the old ones, just with a different twist. It reminds me of poor John Garfield—please excuse the pronunciation, again—who was literally destroyed, simply torn to pieces. He was so good-looking, so sexy, but they had to go and accuse him of being a communist. It gives me goose bumps. I know that honesty does not have any intrinsic merit. And old age and its various aches and pains have a way of turning a person into a coward—who am I kidding, anyway? But since these girls kept harping away that I had to record my story on the tape recorder, I gave it some thought and made my decision. No matter how embarrassing it would be, no matter how many reasons my sisters would now have to boo and hiss at me (I've certainly made it easy for them), what I want to do is save my skin, because I don't have any other choice.

These girls tell me to get off my high horse with the honesty routine. They tell me to quit bluffing—they say I have to have *some* kind of vice, especially in the neighborhood I live in. I live in Moratalaz, for the record, in Arroyo Fontarrón, a neighborhood of modest apartments, but at least I have a roof over my head, somewhere to watch movies on TV, somewhere to reread my old, bound copies of *Fotogramas*, somewhere to dream. But they look at me and think that when I go out at night or in the daytime to walk my dogs, with all the unemployed types in the neighborhood, in the empty lots between Moratalaz and Vallecas, in the cheap neighborhood movie houses, in the toilets at the supermarket, there's always some desperate soul to pick up if you're desperate enough yourself. That is what they say to me, but they're wrong. Honestly, they're dead wrong, and that doesn't mean I'm happy about it, but I must be honest and straightforward to the end.

The truth is, Mr. Policeman, I would be thrilled to be able to tell you stories as wild as theirs, I would give anything for it to be true, and I certainly don't want you to think that I'm a prude, or repressed, or voluntarily chaste, or a penitent of the brotherhood of the Holy Chastity Belt of Christ. Nothing of the sort. If I don't practice the craft, it's simply because I can't, even though I'm dying to. Things are what they are. Is that honest enough for you? I imagine that facts are what you care about, not imitations. I mean, intentions. Intentions. Occasionally I have slips of the tongue. And when it comes to facts, I swear to you I'm clean. Diaphanous. Oh, what I wouldn't give to be able to tell you about my latest tumbles, like in the old days, in my better years—and I did have better years, oh did I have them. They were the magnificent, rollicking days of champions, although I do imagine that my crimes predate your laws—that is to say, that my crimes don't count, because they are prehistoric by now. Oh, it's so depressing, and it makes me even more depressed to think back on them now. Maybe the other girls can look back, maybe they speak of things that happened to them as children as if they happened just yesterday, and I imagine they've garnished them somewhat—after all, queers have a tendency toward exaggeration, always wanting to shock and make people think that their lives are filled with outlandish, wild behavior all the time. To each her own. They are made of martyr's blood or perhaps they think themselves immune, but wild fantasies—no offense, Mr. Policeman—have a terribly strong effect on me, and I prefer to tell things the way they are.

Wouldn't it be amusing if I—a poor soul without a cent to my name, certainly not enough to catch the Contour, or whatever they call that big, fast French plane that can whip you over to Japan in a couple of minutes—were to be the first, if not the last, to fall? All because I have tried not to boast of things I do not do, those things that do not penetrate me, that I do not suck off, in my attempt to prove myself a modern-day Joan of Arc. It would be unjust, not to mention incompetent and senseless, and I think I deserve respect and consideration for my stance, and nobody has the right to call me indulgent or frightened.

These girls tell me to stop crying like a man and behave like a real woman. Oh how I would love that. I would
give my entire collection of *Fotogramas* to be able to exercise true womanhood. But then if I had the means, the hair,
and the health to behave like a true feminine soul, like I did
in my more prosperous years, those old copies of *Fotogramas*
wouldn't be so important to me now. Nor so very necessary.
But you must know that I am prepared to tell you the whole
truth, and I hope you understand and take that into account.

Just so these girls don't claim that I've deliberately left
certain things out, I shall tell you about my most recent incident, a very special exception, believe me, and you will see
that it is a terribly sad tale. As they say, the skinny dogs
always catch the most fleas, and in this case truer words have
never been spoken. Just picture it. My sexual drive had been
all but numbed from lack of practice. Then, finally, the
moment arrived, but by then I had gone so long without
(that is, without action) that I no longer even suffered; why,
I hardly felt anything at all. I just walked through life in this
aspect like a zombie, a pillow—I had even lost interest in
the cheap thrill of looking at other people, so as to avoid the
inevitable letdown, the depression that comes from looking
and not touching. And so I have become a discreet, modest
queer—and by "modest" I mean that I don't even lift my gaze
up from the ground below me. I never look at anything more
than the ankles of the people passing by—feet have never
been a particular fetish for me, not like for some people. I
have one friend, a painter, who has a coronary every time
she spots a tempting pair of feet. They call her the Foot

Faggot, even in the art books and catalogs—her last exhi-
bition was so full of feet, feet everywhere, in every possible
position, that by the time you were through you had bun-
ions. Of course, I only go to art exhibits if I can get in for
free. Well anyway, that has never been a vice of mine. I walk
along the street with my eyes downcast, quite contentedly,
never thinking the least little thing of the men that cross my
path. But one afternoon, as night fell, I was just coming back
from a walk with Poli and Fairie when I saw that a young
man had been following my footsteps. You might ask how
I could have noticed this, given that I walk through life with
my eyes glued to the ground, and I'll tell you, to clear my
name: my sudden admirer was a midget. A real midget. Like
the kind in the circus. Given his size, obviously, he fit into
my field of vision more fully that most. And among other
things, what I saw was a lump under his zipper that, after
tea time, practically grazed the ground. You can imagine
what went through my mind: that this guy's vertical short-
comings were more than compensated for in the horizon-
tal. And on top of it, the eyes that gazed up at me were filled
with desire. I practically toppled over in my high heels from
the surprise, because as it turned out, he wasn't bad-looking
at all. He was, however, a little hunchbacked and had a
strange, sort of half-baked voice, and so after the initial
shock, he did gross me out a bit, despite my desperate state.
But he kept on looking at me, persistent and leery, and
quickly asked me something about my dogs—a handy excuse—and then invited me to partake in one of his Camel
Lights. Then he asked me out for a cup of coffee and I said

"of course"—after all, my stomach was growling by then. We went to a bar, and I must admit I was a bit hesitant about being seen in such company. Now, I know that is not a very kind thought, and I said to myself don't be so petty, sleep with him if you need to, poor thing, he looks like he could use some affection. Surely he was as deprived as I was—I mean, we were made for each other. He put his hand on my knee first and then on my thigh, pressing down on them, and when the conversation waned he very naturally flipped through the newspapers he was carrying. One of them opened to an article on South Africa—an article on discrimination. And I couldn't reject him, as repugnant as he was to me, because then the poor thing would think that I was a racist. And so there I was, caught in a diplomatic dilemma, not knowing what to do: on the one hand, my nether regions had begun to purr from the sexual hunger that couldn't help but be awakened by my admirer's caresses; but on the other hand, the little hunchback did make my flesh crawl a bit, and then to top it off, all those newspapers with those screaming headlines about racism and marginalization. And so, when he asked me the classic question ("Is there somewhere we can go?"), I said yes, I live alone, we can go to my house for a little while if you'd like, I live close by. But I swear, Mr. Policeman, I had to muster up every last bit of courage to say that and to remind myself that it was an act of charity on my part. Then, Mr. Policeman, get this: he said,

"All right, if that's what you want, but I should tell you something first." And I said,

"Tell me." And suddenly he got all Marlon Brando on me and said, straight out:

"I charge for this kind of thing, you know?"

Now, if these ladies here are going to tell me that the law might take issue with this, and invoke the same chauvinistic, reactionary laws that you have enacted to abuse the queer population, forget it. It's simply not just, for one thing, but even if it were, I would have to be the very last on your list. Don't tell me that I haven't already broken the record for the title and crown of the most downtrodden, world-weary queer in existence.

Because moreover, I couldn't look like a poor little nobody. I had to give him the usual routine that I was out of cash, that they were sending me a new ATM card, et cetera. Then, to add insult to injury, Mr. Quasimodo said his good-bye with a quick, "Okay, some other time then, sorry about that. But you're the one who's missing out. You don't know what you're missing, in fact." What a nerve.

The truth is, it all sounds like a big joke now, but at the time I was so distraught that I went running home, completely traumatized and desperate to simply cry my eyes out. And I thought of how that hunchback could at least afford to take a course in personality improvement, or rebirthing, while I was as miserable as a drowned rat. I had to live with my complexes and neuroses, with no escape or solace other than my bound collection—God bless it—of *Fotogramas*.

The first copy I have is from 1946, the magazine's inaugural year, which features a sepia-tint photo of the movie *Tortilla Flat*, with Spencer Tracy, Hedy Lamarr, and John

Garfield, who is worth his weight in gold. Two such different yet consummately attractive men, one who seduces you with his goodness, the other with his careless charisma. And that gorgeous woman between the two of them, with those succulent lips, my God, all I had to do was close my eyes and I became Hedy Lamarr. I had to hold back my laughter so as not to ruin the scene, because Garfield somehow managed to wiggle his finger underneath my panties without anyone noticing while I, with my left arm on my hip, restrained myself as I held Spencer's magic wand on my right side. Spencer, of course, had a whole different drama going on—meaning his shenanigans with Katharine Hepburn.

I watched *Tortilla Flat* quite recently, I think, though I don't know for sure because it seems that I've simply lost my memory when it comes to the movies; I couldn't tell you the full story of one single film from start to finish. It must be the lack of circulation in the brain that comes from old age, or maybe my lack of sexual activity. It's a good thing I have my *Fotogramas*, with all those marvelous photographs.

And then there's the photo of Guy Madison, dressed up like a sailor in *Since You Went Away*, which I cut out and framed because I can't stand saving old bits of paper. I've spent so many unforgettable nights with that photograph, transformed into a woman of the world, a woman who needed a sailor like him, at a certain moment in her life, a sailor with that blond hair and sweet smile and those honest, hardworking hands that knew so very well how to caress a woman. After I'd lowered his trousers, I would lick off every last bit of saltwater from his body.

For a different kind of thrill, there was the photo of Joel McCrea and Anthony Quinn in *Buffalo Bill*. Joel is the protagonist and Quinn the Indian chief, and in the photo it appears beyond question that Joel is copping a feel underneath Anthony's lower braids. The two of them are looking in the same direction—toward me, of course, a beautiful Indian woman, completely nude and tied to a post, my legs slightly open, the trophy over whom the two of them will fight to the death. No matter how many times I look at that photograph I can never decide which one of them I want more, and so I keep the two of them fighting and fighting, and with all that muscle and blood dancing before me, I can't stand the indecision any longer and end up calling in a spectacular Indian man who has been watching the battle, so that he can savagely have his way with me. And he does.

On the other hand—and I don't know why—I always end up being the one to savagely defile Rory Calhoun, in the photo where he is shown practicing his boxing moves in a movie that was called *Nob Hill* in English—*Fotogramas* doesn't give it a name in Spanish. Rory is naked from the waist up, wearing a kind of tight pajama bottom—I use a magnifying glass to examine his package close up. But there's nothing doing; with athletes it's always the same thing—they get scared off by their fans and won't give you a fuck, not even if you threaten to kill them. Another one like that is Burt Lancaster in *The Killers*, where he, too, plays a boxer. There's a photo of him—my God, just looking at it is enough to make you come. And the same goes for another actor, not quite so well-known, the adorable Bill Williams—

a beautiful, well-coiffed, healthy-faced champion, in the RKO movie *Till the End of Time*. Every time I would go and see the three of them—each in his respective movie, of course—I would put on a very well-cut suit with my little mane all slicked down, and I wouldn't stop until I convinced them to come over to my apartment, the apartment of an independent woman with a past. But once we arrived there, it was always the same old story: they would always insist on saving their energy for the boxing ring. My last resort was always to slip something into their mineral water to make them sleep, and then I would take off their clothes and chain them to the bed, using the sheets to tie them down. And then I would mount them as they woke up and have my way with them, like a real pervert, until I was good and satisfied.

The only one I never had to try very hard with was Tarzan—the Tarzan I like, Johnny Weissmuller, a saucy little exhibitionist. What a screamer, and not just when he was swinging from one tree to another, either—whenever he came he would scream like hell. Sometimes I would get so embarrassed I would cover his mouth as my canal was spread wide open by that unbelievable angel's machete. And then I would turn to him in anguish and say, "Tarzan, good God, control yourself, everyone can hear us." And I followed him, devoted, through the jungle, without a thought to the expense, and he always found the time to fix my skins. The negative side of it all was that he began to develop a very unpleasant predilection—he would turn up with his little son, wanting a ménage à trois, and I've never had a thing for little boys; I'm no molester, like some people I know, who go on those maternal kicks just so they can cruise boys, like Herodes, who was a born child molester. That was how Tarzan ended up as well, and that was why I finally stopped seeing him.

If you want a good threesome, *Nightmare Alley,* the Fox movie with Tyrone Power, Coleen Gray, and a guy called Mike Mazurki, is a good bet. I have a copy of *Fotogramas* with a shot that just knocks me out, because I am the spitting image of Coleen Gray, who is perched upon Tyrone's thighs. In the same photo, Mike is looking terribly brutish, with a short little tiger skin that offers a perfect outline of his jewels underneath, and the look in his eyes makes it abundantly clear that he's ready to fuck us both—at the same time. I don't know how he manages it, but he always does. And I don't mind at all that Tyrone enjoys it even more than I do.

Of course, the one person I can't bear is that simpy Olivia de Havilland. I have always held a torch for Errol Flynn, especially as Robin Hood. That insipid, mousy Olivia never stops pawing at him throughout the entire film, but *Fotogramas* did do a special retrospective spread with a picture of Errol alone, wounded by an arrow just below his collarbone, and when I saw that shot, I said to myself this is your big chance. I quickly made myself up and once I was dressed to the nines I went running to tend to him. And once his fever had subsided he looked at me and said,

"Who are you? Where on earth is that ridiculous Olivia?" and I said,

"Shh, shh, let's not talk about her, let's talk about us, my love." And then he confessed that he would love to talk but right now, if I didn't mind, he'd rather take a toss in the hay with me. Naturally I was overjoyed, and we did it right there in the barn like a couple of rabbits. Now, I should tell you: those things they say about Flynn, that he's not so well-hung, are absolutely untrue. He's hung all right.

All the actors I like are well-hung. Sometimes, on long winter afternoons, they have welcomed me to their beds, their sheets, their bidets, with the *Fotogramas* magazine between us.

For me, no one can top Aldo Ray in a bathing suit. And then there's Henri Vidal, hard as a rock and fast as a speeding bullet when he takes off that little toga skirt in *Fabiola*. Or Ralph Meeker, whose naked body is worthy of a spread in a gay porno magazine and who lets anyone suck him off, any time of day, no ifs, ands, or buts. Tab Hunter, on the other hand, has a penchant for taking it from behind, but with a little patience you can convince him to change position, and he's no slouch at that, either. Jeffrey Hunter always says that if I let him stick it in a little, he'll give me twenty bucks; what he doesn't realize is that I'd do it for a ham sandwich—but only if he'll promise to stick it in a lot, not just a little. Ben Cooper, whom I first saw in a photo with Anna Magnani in *The Rose Tattoo*, has a tattoo of the Statue of Liberty on his member, which changes color as he pumps me up and down. And there are so many others. So many others who might not be as famous as the great

Hollywood legends, but then again, they're not quite so overexposed either.

The truth is, Mr. Policeman, I can generally do without the big stars, although there have been a few exceptions. I do without them, in the first place, because it would be ludicrous to compete with those powerful actresses, and secondly because the lesser-known actors are easier to persuade; they figure maybe you can help their careers out a little.

Those are the ones who, once I gain their confidence, admit to this. They start out talking a big game about their hit movies, but they inevitably end up pouring their hearts out about their terrible frustrations. That was exactly what happened with a certain Spanish matador, exceptionally good-looking, who made a few movies — *The Last Torch Song,* for example, is one of them, although I preferred him in *Afternoon of the Bulls.* But I eventually lost track of him. I told you before, Mr. Policeman, I don't know what is wrong with me lately, but I simply forget all the plots of these movies — of course, there's no way I could ever forget *Little Women,* but God help me if I had to tell you the storyline of *The Last Torch Song.* When it first came out in my hometown, I think I saw it fifteen times, and that's no exaggeration. I would go to see it with my friend Bayonesa — both of us knew the dialogue by heart, and each time we'd go one of us would play Sara Montiel and the other would act out the other roles. Whenever I played darling Sara's part, my best moments were always during the dialogues with the little bullfighter. And wouldn't you know, the other day I saw it

again, in one of the latest *Fotogramas*, in an article about
sometime actors. My heart leapt the instant I saw him. He's
changed quite a bit, mind you, but even so I got all shivery
and nervous. And I'm not one of those hieroglyphic types,
you know—it's not like I have a thing for older men or anything, but with this man I simply couldn't help myself. I said,
    "Why, aren't you Enrique Vera?" And he looked so
touched by that. Then he invited me to eat at La Dorada—
I wore a very distinguished outfit and he looked like a real
gentleman in his light-colored suit (it was summer), which
he filled out divinely, almost as well as he filled out those
matador outfits he wore on the screen and in the bullring.
He had reserved a private room for the two of us. I asked
him to select the menu but for the life of me I can't remember what we ate, because I immediately began rubbing my
leg up against his and I felt my entire body come alive and
open up as wide as the Portico of the Gloria on Santiago's
feast day. I was in rapture. I flung myself on top of that
matador's steely lance, and he attacked me violently, performing a picture-perfect maneuver worthy of the great
bullfighter Manolete. He turned me around and dazzled me
with his penetration, driving me wild as I oozed happiness
while outside, in the dining rooms, the faint sound of "Matador, matador, matador" could be heard through our cries.
    A dream, Mr. Policeman.
    Nothing more than a dream; I hope you'll forgive me
for getting carried away. These girlfriends of mine, such
adorable things, say it won't make any difference. I know
that can't be true. I think you are a reasonable man. And

this law in question has to have its limits. It must. They tell me no, they tell me that you can just walk right into anyone's house and carry off whomever you find in what you consider a compromising position. That you'll stop at nothing. They say that you respect nothing and no one. Not even dreams, or imagination. They tell me that you have policemen for everything. And I just can't believe that. I've never been to America, but I know it perfectly well. From the movies, that is. And *Fotogramas*. I've seen millions of movies and in the end you always, always turn out to be fair, respectful people, a nation full of freedom and joy. Oh—excuse me, I get excited so easily. I'm not trying to go around preaching to you, God no—who am I to do that? The girls here tell me not to get all worked up, that it doesn't matter, that I've told you enough already. Dreams. Only dreams. And if that law punishes dreams, Mr. Policeman, we might as well end it all right now.

So here you have me. Here I am. Tied to the wooden stake like Jean Seberg in *St. Joan*. It's too late to fix my hair up gamine style, but that doesn't matter. Attitude is what matters here. The gesture. Here you have me. And I shall ask only one favor of you: when you set me on fire, do it with my bound collection of old *Fotogramas*. Please, I even ask this of you in English. Set me on fire with my magazines. Because if what my girlfriends say is true, it is only fair that my *Fotogramas* and I should go down in flames together, because after all, they were what betrayed me in the end.

# VII

*Where Veronica Switchblade,*
*theoretical expert in the art*
*of theater and light comedy,*
*improvises a dramatic monologue*
*to caution the impatient and*
*confound her inquisitors*

Yes, here he sleeps beside me, this white lung that remains blissfully unaware of my insomnia, separated from me by slumber's black abyss, trapped by the other side, held captive by a hungry Morpheus, who is poised to devour him, for his beauty is so great and his innocence so very tempting. He sleeps, unaware that he ignores me — at the very least, one would think his disdain could provide me with some blessing, like the asp that filled Cleopatra's veins with dark joy, like the hemlock that introduced Socrates' deepest death wish into his heart. It is cold, and the silence is as inflamed as a sickly muscle, and yet I have no one to console me. He sleeps like an angel after the battle, after banishing an army of devils into hell, and now he breathes so calmly, almost cautiously, as if wading through a river naked, submerged in murky waters up to his chest.

His body is on fire. Yesterday he said to me, "You
don't know how much you remind me of my first girlfriend"—that is, the first girl he ever loved. He still car-
ries her photograph in his wallet, and every time he gazes
at it, his eyes brim over with melancholy tears. "You can't
imagine the tasty little crack between her legs," he says to
me in the youthful tones of the working class. That crack,
as he calls it, is what he misses the most. A poor boy of such
ever-changing beauty—there are moments when he is as
delicate and misty as Donatello's *David*, and then he can
become as surly and cutting as a young man on the streets
of Mamma Roma, a poor, sweet little puppy braving the
elements, at the mercy of all the hungry wolves in the big
city, expelled from the tender genital crevice of his first
beloved, by the brio of his own budding youth. His body
is on fire but his flame will never burn inside of me, for he
believes that my fortune is that of a woman, and I, unfortunate soul that I am, must ensure that he continues to
believe this, so that he won't abandon me. Lying beneath
him I must feign the sacred heights of pleasure, I must
convince him that he has discovered my secret paradise,
after so many years of deriving ecstasy from that odious
place, after having reveled in so much pleasure from that
tiny cavity that has been the recipient of such abundant
live flesh, war-hungry meat, and animal ferocity. He continues to sleep and I don't dare stir, oh complicit shadows,
to wipe my deceitful secret with soft cotton, and remove
the thick deluge of his aromatic semen, the joyous genital
lava that he poured inside of me only an hour ago (or was

it perhaps a century?), amid moans, hoarse declarations of love, and promises of eternal devotion. Because you, he said to me, you are a woman from the tips of your fingers down to the marrow of your bones. You, I tell myself, are finally the woman he wants you to be — the woman that he needs, poor, adoring fool that he is.

Shakespeare himself could never have envisioned such misfortune. The tragic heroism of Hamlet pales in comparison — why, that work of drama would have been relegated to second-tier material for the world's great repertory troupes once they heard the soliloquy that the Bard of Stratford would have composed upon hearing my lamentations. Othello's envy would never have inspired such reverence in the Albion theater on so many different occasions, nor would Segismundo's torment, in the amphitheater at Almagro, have rocked the peaceful existence of La Mancha quite so brutally as my misfortune. Oh, but I was born centuries too late, and I discovered the muses of the theater far too late as well. Destiny made its unfortunate arrival in my entrails through the blackened corridors that rise in the west, and a capricious Mother Nature raised an impenetrable barrier in the place where my grand portal should have been. Everything has proved useless: the ingenuity and cleverness of experts, the skill of surgeons, the voracity of every imaginable sort of intermediary, the advice of urologists, to say nothing of the dubious but comforting assurances of a clinic in Casablanca where I spent four months. There in Casablanca, I laid prostrate on an operating table for four hours as I fervently renounced my misbegotten attribute and desperately embraced

the dream of a free and complete womanhood with the fingers of my desire and the force of my illusions.

I traveled to Casablanca and paid the extravagant costs
of an operation with the money I earned from the Calderón
de la Barca theatrical prize, a prize that was mysteriously
awarded to me by a group of (perhaps inebriated) judges
for the tragedy I wrote in homage to Hecate, one of Macbeth's
witches. Of course, when I won the award I was already
swimming in debt, but the greatest creditor on earth is an
elusive thing called happiness and the intangible privilege
of being content with oneself. And then, oh, the sadness of
this archangel that now sleeps beside me, frustrated by his
own impotence at the moment in which he was about to
hungrily enter my hindmost treasures. My beautiful young
friend, you see, was stricken by a mysterious syndrome
developed after so many unspeakable experiences he endured at the hands of certain artisans of the craft, if "craft"
can be considered the proper word for the decadent and
abusive filth that they brew and imbibe.

It has been a long, perilous road, but when I gazed on
the splendor of my young man I felt my suffering redeemed
in his gleeful incredulity, his urgency to try me after I finally
revealed my new jewel, the glimmering channel that a precision scalpel had chiseled between my thighs several weeks
earlier in a distant country amid accusatory glares and enig-
matic words, amid the fluctuating effects of anesthesia, all
in the capricious hands of fate. Thank heavens I emerged
safely and my precious furrow, though I envisioned it to be
consummately sensitive, delicate, and fecund, like a rare

orchid entrusted to the loving care of a geisha, at least had a tremulous, succulent, promising look to it. My happiness, however, was short-lived, oh shadows that protect the fires of my mind, and the reality that awaited me was as hard as flint.

I asked the man who now sleeps beside me, unaware of my anguish, not to be violent, not to demand everything all at once, for my flower was still quite tender and the anxiousness of his lips and the increasing impatience of his flaming rod, rigid as a unicorn's horn, could ruin everything. A useless precaution, oh darkness that invades my soul, for the rough, dry quality of my spurious marvel could only have been fashioned with waste materials. Specifically, I believe it has been fashioned out of vinyl, a material as cheap and common as they come, because what else could explain such dryness, such stiffness, such total and complete absence of pleasure? My young man pounced upon it like a shipwreck victim who clings to the life raft that appears, like magic, in the middle of a storm. He seemed ready to devour it, willing to destroy his tongue in that series of folds that, to me, felt like aluminum or asbestos, even though to him, in the dim light, it seemed moist and as golden as sponge cake. I cried with pleasure during the first few seconds, very real cries, because my desire for happiness was so very ripe, like a pomegranate bursting forth with its dark red juice. But I quickly realized that it was all an illusion, a fantasy that had burgeoned from my own deep need, the painful inertia of my determination to be a woman for him. I wanted to rescue him from his well of apathy, I wanted to redeem all the terrible nightmares he suffered on account of the genital deviance of a certain extraordinary writer and, after that, a second-rate poet, a nymphomaniac art critic, a painter enslaved by his own inflamed orgasms, and a film director intent on nursing his psyche with the phalluses of the young men who passed through his life. That was when I understood that the bedouin doctor had made a small fortune at my expense, sewing me up with a polyester vagina instead of the mahogany I had been promised. And I lacked the courage to tell my little cherub, who swore that I drove him wild, as he assaulted my dead-end alley with his tongue, with his frenetic and ultimately pointless resolve to bring me to the fields of Eden.

When I met him, he was homeless and hungry; he told me he wanted nothing to do with intellectuals, he'd had more than enough of them. I offered him my home and a cot in the extra room and he said that he would accept my offer only if I promised not to molest him later on. Then he asked me a rather strange question:

"Are there a lot of ashtrays in this house?"

He was very suspicious of ashtrays—the minute you make a wrong move, they betray you, he said. I suppose the hunger and fatigue had made him delirious, but I calmed him down, assuring him that since neither of us smoked, we would take all the ashtrays in the house and lock them away somewhere. He has been living with me ever since then, as glued to me as my own misfortune, and he lives as deeply inside of me as my own tenderness, confiding in me all the defects of his character and all the errors he has made in his life.

He once told me about a celebrated poet who proposed they play a strange, complicated game: he was to appear at a poetry reading and claim that he was a fledgling poet named Serafín Bruñido and that he had written three hermetic poems in *Posterior Poetry*, an anthology assembled by the celebrated poet. My beautiful friend, newly baptized as the seraphic Serafín, wanted to know the true author of these three hermetic poems, and the celebrated poet sardonically replied that it was "heteronomous, my young friend; he wanders around aimlessly like a soul in purgatory, like a wild dybbuk, looking for a beautiful, genteel body to inhabit." And then he said to my friend that he had been bestowed the great fortune of serving as the "host" of this anonymous scribe. My friend took this to mean something very important—after all, the celebrated poet was handing him a brilliant opportunity on a silver platter. It was rather odd, no doubt, but the celebrated poet claimed that this was his way—an oblique way—of making love, and he asked for nothing in exchange.

From the hands of this poetic predator—exquisite hands covered in rings—my beautiful friend was given over to the hands of a huntress, a woman who wrote bold, shocking verses, and who always wore men's gloves. She never took them off, not even in the shower. She and my friend took showers together on several occasions, but the lady poet would never allow him to exert his manhood with her. Amid the swirls of steam rising up from the hot water, the two of them would wrap themselves in thick ivory towels and pretend to be teenage lesbians, kissing delicately on the lips as if afraid of hurting each other. Slowly they kissed each other's necks, shoulders, underarms, but according to my beautiful friend, no matter how hard he tried he couldn't fulfill his manly desires with her—it was as if that steam cloud was infused with some kind of drug, it felt as if the lady poet had put some kind of mysterious herbs in the water heater. He said it felt as though they were anesthetized, their muscles numbed, as if they moved within an odd veil of pleasure that prevented my friend from exercising his manhood no matter how hard he tried, no matter how he attempted to enter her and satisfy his strong urges, for the lady poet had the body of a lovely little girl. Her breasts were like apricots, her thighs long and supple, and her sex was as soft as the oily feathers of a newborn sparrow. But she only wanted him to kiss her sex, nothing more, and fashioned a turban out of the towel, which she placed upon him as he kneeled at her feet. In his ear she whispered, "My little tart," and she stroked his ass with consummate tenderness despite the men's gloves she wore, and whispered to him things like "My love, my deviant little girl, my little Sappho." The truth is, he liked what he saw, he liked the lady poet's wet, nude body, even though it didn't thrill him the way a man's body did. She said to him, in a very low voice, "Don't fool yourself, my love, you are like me, we're identical," and they kissed one another for hours as if kissing before a mirror.

Literary types are an odd bunch, says my friend who now sleeps beside me with his member tucked between his legs, like a snake resting in the sweet slumber of hibernation, satisfied from the pleasure he thinks he has given me.

The celebrated poet, dressed up in a black *djellaba*, used to make him lie down on a chaise as he recited the verses of Catullus. Standing upright, the celebrated poet would grow harder and harder until finally, in a state of extreme arousal, he would ask my friend to touch him. My friend would oblige, and as he touched the tip of that black tent, barely grazing it with his fingertip, he could nonetheless feel the material grow thick with very intellectual semen. That was oblique sex, the poet said, the sex of *Posterior Poetry*. Parabolic, cheap sex. The girl with the gloves, on the other hand, made my friend feel like her little sister and he became so confused that he no longer knew where the spurts of pleasure came from, those immense cramps of pleasure that shot out from his stomach up to his ears and down through to his heels. His cock was still totally soft but he ejaculated anyway, and the ecstasy was so intense that it felt almost dangerous, something that couldn't possibly be good, just as the frenzy of the girl with the gloves couldn't possibly be good either, nor her final spasms, nor the desperation with which she embraced him as she said, "You are my master, my mistress, my torment." And then later on in the bedroom, after having slept a bit, she insisted on dressing him in her very masculine suits, which made him feel as though he was her prisoner.

"Don't forget," the girl with the gloves warned him as he left, "your name is Rosaura Mask."

It was enough to drive him insane, said the boy who now sleeps beside me, the boy who thinks that in me he has finally found a normal woman. The boy who once, in a fit of gratitude, tried to bring me ecstasy in my old pleasure spot, where my soul takes the shape of a drain and contracts like a suspicious mollusk, like a carnivorous plant, like a bruised eyelid. And he cried over his failure like a seminarian expelled from the monastery because of poor health, like a long-distance runner forced to abandon the race at the final round. He hugged me tightly from behind and cried like a baby for having failed, and cursed those people who taught him such twisted forms of love, and swore that he loved me as he had never loved anyone else before.

How could I not sacrifice everything for him, for a love like that? Why, I would sacrifice my life if I had to. I was sick of all the one-night stands, I was exhausted from cruising the crowded catacombs like a hungry jackal, and I had grown wise to the sudden gleam of the switchblades that so often came after me, motivated by envy, avarice, or madness. That was what led me to Casablanca. And I found him here, in the vulnerable but warm harbor of love, and I came looking for him with the anguished joy of a boat heading for dry land after the terrible fear of being shipwrecked. This is where I found him, and he remains true to me, always at my side.

He sleeps now. It is cold and the color of the night is the color of the final hours. I won't arise, oh vigilant shadows, and I will allow this sweet boy's semen to grow dry so that nothing else may blossom except his will to live, his will that has been so terribly damaged by so many hungry wolves. I want him to have sweet dreams, far from the anal demands of this Good Samaritan, far from his old impotence and his threatening dysphasia, far from all posterior poetry and gloves like masks, and safe from the inflamed orgasms of a neo-Expressionist of the Huelva artistic school, the insatiable throat of an expert in the art of Juan Gris, the abscesses and the cavities of a movie director who required his help with screenplays, and safe from a pale, obese young girl who drank in hope as she drank from his creamy fountain of inspiration. The air is cold, oh intimate darkness, and my body is frozen while this angel whom I shepherd smolders in the warm bonfire of his dream life.

Perhaps the day will come when my heart is able to open wide once again. When that day comes I will return to Casablanca and hunt down the surgeon who defrauded me, and I will rip out his private parts with my bare teeth and force him to attach his dismembered sex to the place where he destroyed me. And if someone, oh vengeful shadows, if one of those newfangled inquisitors threatens me with prison or torture for once again being able to derive joy a posteriori, I will do everything I can to force that Casablanca surgeon to rip out his pendulous policeman's jewels and replace them with a pair of plastic sacs, and I will sew on his future misery with steel twine, because that is what he deserves for refusing to understand the pain, the hopes, and the anguish of those condemned to love with their backs turned.

# Epilogue

*Where Miss Boccaccio
explains her emotional state after
such extensive use, and how she
now quivers in the knowledge
of an obligation fulfilled*

Sore. My back door is horribly sore and chafed from the dispatches of these seven wayward women. Of course, when it was over, they all complained like a bunch of cockatoos because they didn't like how it came out, because they didn't have enough time to rehearse, and they were all ready to redo their speeches. Thank God my owner stepped in and said nothing doing. She, in fact, was the first one to say she didn't like how her presentation came off but it was much better that way, she said, for it was more spontaneous, more sincere and thought-provoking. And my owner simply loves to be provocative—good lord, she is a born provocateur. She should have dedicated her life to giving speeches in the Parliament instead of dancing in variety shows.

My owner, Miss Madelon, lubricated my inner machine with the most expensive oils because by the end I was screeching so terribly it hurt to listen to me; the back-door batteries got the best of me and this humble servant now has a vagina covered in sores.

"You weak little cunt," Mercurio spat at me with scorn. "I'd be ashamed to have as little stamina as you."

Miss Mercurio's problem, of course, is that she's out for blood because she didn't get any action at all. And it seems as if everyone had conspired together on that one. Maybe Sindo will call tomorrow, Sunday, but he might also have gotten discharged by now, and Totana the redhead might not be bold enough to call. That jai-alai player has a contract in Tijuana, and the soccer player from the Canary Islands, the one who plays for Vallecano, will already be back home on his island, having found a Swedish retiree who can lick his sadness away. Of course, Madelon's dry spell won't last for long, she's quite a girl, but Miss Mercurio has most definitely picked up that menopause syndrome. I can just picture her during all those lonely nights, telling herself over and over again that she is finished as a woman and forcing the plug of the telephone jack, as if that would help her, at her age, to soften her stiffened organs.

"Whoever invented that saying about how God gives bread to those who have no teeth was so very wise," Mercurio says to me, her mood embittered by her suspicion and mistrust.

I, however, am dancing on air, resplendent—never better, in fact. My mood is not the least bit shrill or frayed. Honestly. I feel like a real militant, the most militant queer in the world. Boccaccio the warrior woman, that's how I feel.

And maybe Mercurio has a point, that my teeth don't have the power to bite, but the way I feel now, I could suck off the Eiffel Tower until it melted away to nothing at all.

With my owner at my side, we replayed all the cassettes. And if the police chief of the State of Georgia, where they enact such "homocidal" laws, doesn't have a change of heart when he hears them, it's because he's had a stroke, or a lobotomy. Just as Colette la Coco says, this is a veritable manifesto, although of course she would have made it far more concise. That woman is going to end her days fucking by fax, I swear.

I have listened to all the cassettes and the truth is, I am unbelievably aroused. My owner has given me a period of rest, but now what I need, more than the air I breathe, is for someone to plunge more batteries inside of me. There is no question: I am a tape recorder with a veritable uterine furor, and this will be my blessing and my curse for the rest of my days.

This will be my blessing and my curse for as long as I can keep body and soul together. According to that filthy gossip Mercurio, of course, my body is not going to hold together much longer, and maybe she's right, because the feedback that echoes out from my nether regions is something fierce, and maybe I shouldn't fool myself about my health, for better or for worse. And after all I'm neither suicidal nor hypodermic (as Pamela Poodle misguidedly calls it). But who knows; any moment now I might have a little explosion and all of a sudden my little cunt will stop working, indicating that they may as well not bother stick-

ing any more batteries inside of me. That is, unless there
exists a battery that can only get off by sticking it to a dead
machine. If it exists, give it to me, yes, absolutely; if there's
one thing I've learned from these seven lunatics it is the joy
of giving pleasure to someone—or something—else.

To give pleasure to those who appreciate it, and to give
it any way you can, that is the best way to feed the hungry,
sate the thirsty, dress the naked, to teach the ignorant, cure
the sick, and console the grieving. It's the very same thing—
though far more amusing, of course.

I think that this is something Mr. Police Chief of Georgia has to understand—and if not, he can fuck himself.

My owner has organized all the cassettes alphabetically. She is so scrupulous when it comes to this sort of thing;
it's a professional idiosyncrasy of hers. Nobody should shine
brighter than any of the rest. Nobody is to be highlighted
as extra-special. All are to be judged as equals, following the
order of the alphabet. She's put it all together in an adorable package, although in the post office, apparently, they
made a terrible fuss over the thing, because sending an international package involves so many papers, so many security checks. Naturally, my owner assured them that the
package contained nothing more than a few simple, discreet
little cassettes. "Music cassettes," she put on the label. And
those dim-witted customs agents didn't suspect for a second
that in fact, those little cassettes contained pure dynamite.

The cassettes are arranged alphabetically, as a matter
of principle and as a testament to the honor of the sender, a
true professional in the world of entertainment. The police

chief of the State of Georgia, of course, can listen to them in whatever order he wishes. It doesn't matter much, though, because he's going to get quite a shock no matter what he listens to first. What a thrill. I'm sure that for the translation, he'll contract the services of some dark little Puerto Rican, and I'm also sure that the two of them will end up taking a tumble, locked in a sixty-nine in the park just outside the police station.

And you, my girls, I exhort you to do the same. Listen to the cassettes in whichever order you choose: as Pamela Poodle would say, it is irreverent. And Miss Mercurio, who is ready to have a cow, will say, "You mean irrelevant, Pamela dear," but Pamela will say she doesn't care, the words are syllogisms. And in the end, it doesn't matter. The sequence of the individual products has no effect on their cumulative result. Here they are. Seven. You can use me—please use me, please. Stick those batteries in, those batteries that take hours to wear out. Like I said before, the act of giving pleasure is an act of mercy. Have mercy on me. Even if I quiver like a vibrator in an all-girls' school. You can be sure that they will be quivers of satisfaction. Even if I shriek a little with feedback, who cares? I won't give in to the chafing.

Seven of them. Seven against Georgia. Seven little queers, seven cassettes, seven stories, seven screams like seven daggers.